Weather
or Not

Collect all the books in the Luna Bay *series*

*coming soon

Luna Bay

a ♥ ROXY GiRL series

BOOK THREE

Weather or Not

by Francess Lantz

HarperEntertainment
An Imprint of HarperCollinsPublishers

This book is a work of fiction. References to real people, events, establishments, organizations, or locales are intended only to provide a sense of authenticity, and are used fictitiously. All other characters, and all incidents and dialogue, are drawn from the author's imagination and are not to be construed as real.

LUNA BAY: WEATHER OR NOT. Copyright © 2003 by Quiksilver, Inc. All rights reserved. Printed in the United States of America. No part of this book may be used or reproduced in any manner whatsoever without written permission except in the case of brief quotations embodied in critical articles and reviews. For information address HarperCollins Publishers Inc., 10 East 53rd Street, New York, NY 10022.

HarperCollins books are available at special quantity discounts for bulk purchases for sales promotions, premiums, or fundraising. For information please call or write: Special Markets Department, HarperCollins Publishers Inc., 10 East 53rd Street, New York, NY 10022. Telephone (212) 207-7528. Fax: (212) 207-7222.

FIRST EDITION

Designed by Jackie McKee

ISBN 0-06-054837-1

❖ 10 9 8 7 6 5 4 3 2 1

For Lia and Geoff

Acknowledgments

With thanks to Cricket Pechstein, Matt Kechele, Jeffery McGraw, Matt Jacobson, Danielle Beck, and Kendra Marcus.

1

Kanani gazes out the airplane window at what looks like puffy white cotton below. How incredible to be floating in a steel ship, miles and miles above the ground—even higher than the clouds!

Oh, sure, there's a scientific explanation for it all, but Kanani isn't interested in it at the moment. She prefers to let herself be awed by the sheer wonder of the experience.

I'm sailing through the sky at something like five hundred miles per hour! she tells herself. *How amazing is that?*

Next to her, her friends Luna and Rae are having a very different experience.

"These seats are designed for midgets," Luna grumbles, stretching her long, willowy legs into the aisle.

"When I was ten, my grandparents took my sister and me to London," Rae says. "Now *that* was sweet! We flew first class both ways. Plenty of room, great food, free video games . . ."

A flight attendant appears, pushing a cart of lunch trays down the aisle. "Sorry, hon," she tells Luna, "I'm going to have to ask you to move your legs."

Luna groans. "I'm getting claustrophobic."

"At least you're on the aisle," Rae mutters. "I'm stuck here in the middle. I feel like a sardine."

"Pasta or chicken?" the flight attendant asks pleasantly.

"Chicken, I guess," Luna answers halfheartedly. The flight attendant places a plastic tray in front of her. Luna gingerly peels back the foil and wrinkles her nose. "What I wouldn't give for a Surf-N-Taco Burrito Grande right now!"

"Pasta, please," Kanani says. She pulls the foil off her tray like a kid opening a Christmas present. The food looks okay to her, and she loves the little individually wrapped packages of crackers and cheese, salad dressing, and cookies. She unwraps her plastic fork and takes a bite.

"You actually like that glop?" Luna asks, eyeing her skeptically.

Kanani shrugs. How can she explain? "I've never been on an airplane before," she says, "except when my birthmother took me from Hawaii to California. But I was only a month old, so I don't remember that."

"What Kanani is trying to say," interrupts Luna's mother, Cate, from the row behind them, "is that she's not jaded like the two of you."

"Hey, just because I don't like airplane food doesn't mean I'm jaded," Luna says indignantly. "I'm totally stoked about this trip. You know that, Mom."

"Well, let's hope so," Luna's father, Tuck, pipes up. "Sebastian Inlet is the hottest break in Florida. On the entire East Coast, in fact. Any surfer worth his wet suit will tell you so."

"Not only that," Cate adds, "but the Florida Longboard Open is one of the most prestigious contests around. If you shine there, the entire longboarding world takes notice."

"And Kanani's going to shine," Rae says, beaming at her friend.

"Oh, come on," Kanani protests, embarrassed. "You guys are the hot competitors, not me."

Just a couple of months ago, Rae had won second place at the Amateur Surfing Association's Western Championship, and Luna had come in fourth.

"But Luna and Rae aren't longboarders like us," Tuck reminds her. "They know how to shred, sure. But longboarding isn't about shredding. It's about dancing with the wave, feeling the flow. Right, Kanani?"

Kanani nods. Tuck knows what he's talking about. He's been longboarding since the sixties. Usually, he'd rather soul-surf than compete, but a couple of his old buddies from Malibu are running this contest and they invited him to come to Florida and show off his stuff. He agreed, and he's invited Luna's girlfriends to come along.

"So I'm right," Rae says with a nod. "You're going to blow the competition away."

Kanani laughs. Rae has enough competitive drive to power a nuclear submarine. But Kanani's different. The way she sees it, surfing isn't about blowing people away. It isn't about competition at all. It's about having fun, hanging with your crew, and getting in touch with nature.

"Don't laugh," Rae says. "If you win the junior division, you're going to get noticed. You might even attract a sponsor or two."

"Yes, look what happened to Rae after the Western Championship," Cate points out. "Youngest member of the Edge SurfWear surf team! That's a real coup."

Cate casts a meaningful glance at Luna, who pointedly ignores her. Cate Martin was a three-time world champion back in the late seventies and early eighties, and she'd love to have her daughter follow in her footsteps. But Luna isn't totally convinced she wants to go pro. Cate tries to let Luna go her own way, but sometimes she just can't resist giving her a little push.

"Anybody want my OJ?" Kanani asks, trying to change the subject. She knows Luna doesn't want to talk about the competitive surf scene, and to tell the truth, neither does she. The Florida Open will be her first contest, and although she doesn't like to admit it, she's feeling a little nervous. What if she gets out there and chokes? That would be just too embarrassing, especially after Cate and Tuck put up half the money for her airfare. Okay, sure, she's going to pay it back by working in their surf shop this fall. But still, she doesn't want to let them down.

Rae takes the juice, but that doesn't stop her from launching into a big conversation with Luna's mother about the pro scene and how it's changed since Cate was on the tour. Trying to ignore them, Kanani looks out the window at those perfect white clouds and imagines they're puffs of sea foam. Now she's riding her longboard over them, walking to the nose, arching her back and gazing up at the blue, blue sky.

Even hours later, Kanani finds herself still gazing outside, completely in awe of flying so high in the sky. Suddenly, the clouds part and she catches a glimpse of the world down below. She sees lush green fields, a flowing river, pink houses, swaying palm trees. "Look!" she exclaims, pointing out the window. "I think we're in—"

"Ladies and gentlemen," says a crackly voice over the loudspeaker, "we are about to begin our descent into Orlando, Florida. Please return to your seats and keep your seat belts fastened. We should be landing in approximately twenty minutes."

Kanani and her friends let out a collective squeal of excitement.

"Sebastian Inlet, here we come!" Luna cries.

"The West Coast girls are here," Rae declares, "and we're ready to surf!"

Suddenly, Kanani's anxiety evaporates like a jet engine's vapor trail. She's never been in Florida before, or even on the East Coast. Except for that month she spent in Hawaii when she was a newborn, she's never even been outside of southern California! But all that's about to change.

She flips her seat back into the upright position, tightens her seat belt, and declares, "I can hardly wait!"

"Why can't we turn on the air-conditioning?" Luna whines. "It must be over a hundred degrees in here!"

"So open your window," her mother replies.

"It *is* open."

"Come on, Cate," Rae pleads. "We're drowning in a pool of sweat."

Kanani sticks her head out an open window of the rented SUV and lets the breeze blow her thick, chestnut hair. It's hot, all right, and so humid her skin feels sticky, but she doesn't mind. In fact, she kind of likes it.

Maybe it's my Hawaiian heritage, she thinks. *Some of the Hawaiian Islands are hot and humid too.*

"Get used to it, girls," Tuck laughs. "It's August in Florida."

"You'll like it when you hit the surf," Cate says. "No wet suits required."

"I can get behind that," Kanani says. She hates the feel of neoprene against her skin. How much sweeter it will be to feel the cool water and warm sun!

Tuck drives the SUV onto A1A, the elevated highway that traverses the barrier islands off the Florida Atlantic Coast. Kanani gazes out at the shimmering blue water. A big, hawklike bird hovers, then plunges into the sea, emerging with a fish in its mouth.

"An osprey!" Cate exclaims. "Maybe we'll spot one of their nests. They're huge."

"Look!" Luna cries. A sign up ahead says SEBASTIAN INLET, 10 MILES.

Kanani's heart kicks into gear. She's seen photos of the inlet's famous First Peak and she can't wait to experience it for herself.

Luna voices the question they've all been thinking. "Can we hit the water as soon as we get there?"

"Oh, the sacrifices a parent makes for his kid," Tuck says with a laugh.

Cate lets out a melodramatic sigh. "Okay, okay. We'll set up the tents while you girls get wet. But then watch out! We're going to hit the surf with a vengeance. Anyone who gets in our way will eat sand!"

"Ooh, I'm scared," Luna teases as her dad exits the highway and turns into Sebastian Inlet State Park.

He heads straight for the jetties and parks the SUV. The girls strip down to their bathing suits, then jump out and take their boards off the top of the car.

"Whew!" Kanani sighs, wiping droplets of sweat off her forehead. It's even hotter in the sun than it was in the SUV. But she soon forgets the heat when she sees the inlet, the man-made channel where water flows between the two barrier islands. To the west lies the Indian River; to the east, the sparkling aqua blue Atlantic Ocean.

Kanani has read eagerly about the Indian River side of the islands, with its mangrove trees, sea turtles, and manatees. But it's the ocean side that interests her now. With Luna and Rae, she runs toward the jetty—then stops and stares as the famous First Peak comes into view.

"Oh, yeah!" Luna exclaims in an awestruck whisper.

"Sweet," Rae agrees.

Kanani watches as a wave refracts off the jetty and jacks up into a thick four-foot peak. A lucky surfer drops in and settles into the shack—the curling pocket of power just in front of the breaking wave. Then suddenly, the wave slams into Second Peak, launching the surfer into the air before it closes out and slams him into the soup.

"That is some serious surf," Kanani observes.

Luna smiles. "So what are we waiting for?"

"Let's do it!" Rae cries, running toward the water.

Soon they're paddling into the crowded lineup. Luna and Rae are on their shortboards; Kanani is on her favorite nine-foot-one-inch tri-fin. A wave rolls in and Rae goes for it. But two male surfers cut her off, while a third surfer drops into the wave.

"What was that all about?" Luna asks as Rae paddles back to join them.

"Locals only!" a nearby surfer shouts, giving them their answer.

The girls look at each other with uncertainty. Kanani frowns and bites her lip. She's used to Crescent Cove where everyone knows her and respects her ability. Sure, once in a while a group of macho guys will try to snake her waves, but they usually back off when they see that Kanani and her posse—Luna, Rae, and their girlfriends Isobel and Cricket—are serious surfers.

But this is different. How can Kanani and her friends prove themselves if the locals won't even let them catch a wave?

"Hey, check it out," Luna says, nodding in the direction of two twentysomething female surfers.

Kanani smiles. In her experience, girl surfers are usually a little more laid-back and welcoming than the guys.

"Let's go introduce ourselves," Rae suggests.

They paddle over and make eye contact. "Hi," Kanani says, smiling.

One of the girls, a blonde with short, wavy hair, nods. "You girls from around here?"

"California," Luna replies.

"There's plenty of good surf out there," says the other girl, shaking water from her black cornrows. "What do you want with our waves?"

Man, talk about negative vibes! Kanani can feel them radiating off the girls like a toxic heat wave. A set rolls in and the two girls paddle into position. They take off on the same wave, splashing spray at Kanani, Luna, and Rae as they surf by.

"Maybe we should try one of the other breaks farther up the beach," Kanani suggests.

"No way," Rae snaps. "I'm mad now. I'm going to catch a wave or else."

Luna and Kanani exchange a look. When Rae digs in, there's no telling what might happen.

The final wave of the set is rolling in. Rae starts to paddle into position. "Come on," she says. "Take this one with me."

Luna paddles next to Rae. Kanani hangs back, hesitant. She doesn't want to get into a fight with a belligerent local. Then she notices a teenage boy with shaggy blond hair paddling just outside of them. He's in the inside position, which means the wave belongs to him if he wants it, but he may be too far out to catch it.

The wave builds and he paddles hard, but it soon becomes evident he isn't going to make it. That's when he notices Kanani. He catches her eye and grins, showing off a pair of the sweetest dimples she's ever laid eyes on. "Go on, sugar," he drawls. "This one's yours."

"Are you sure?" Kanani stammers. "I mean, I—I—"

"If you waste this wave, you're a fool," he snaps. "Now, get gone, girl!"

Kanani springs into action. Luna and Rae are paddling too, but Kanani's the one in the sweet spot, and as she drops in, she feels herself settle into the pocket. Luna and Rae pull out and now Kanani has the wave to herself—a beautiful open expanse of blue that makes her heart soar. She rockets down the line, crouching to build speed.

Then suddenly, the wave collides with a Second Peak breaker and, with a shriek of joy and surrender, she flies off her board and lands headfirst in the spin cycle.

Hmm, she thinks as the white water works her over, *maybe these Sebastian Inlet locals aren't so bad after all.*

2

Kanani pops up from the white water and paddles back into the lineup. She looks around for the boy who gave her the wave, but Luna and Rae intercept her.

"Was that as much fun as it looked?" Luna asks with a grin.

"Even better. I—"

"How did you do that?" Rae breaks in impatiently. "You were in the perfect spot!"

"True," Kanani agrees, "but I probably wouldn't have had the courage to go if that surfer hadn't yelled at me."

"He yelled at you?" Rae asks, her eyes narrowing.

"Not that kind of yelling," Kanani explains. "He told me the wave was mine. He said, 'Get gone, girl!' So I went."

"Well, where is he?" Luna asks. "We have to thank him."

Kanani searches the water, but the surfer was nowhere in sight. "Maybe he went in," she says. Disappointment tugs at her. There is something about that boy that brings a smile to her face. She wants to see him—and those amazing dimples—again.

"Heads up," Luna says, gesturing toward an incoming set.

The girls paddle into position, eager to see if Kanani's ride has changed the attitude of the locals. They find out almost immediately that it has. Although the surfers are still aggressively jockeying for position, no one actually prevents the girls from taking off. As a result, all three of them are soon catching hot First Peak crushers.

Later, Tuck and Cate come out to join them. A couple of the older surfers in the lineup know Tuck, and a few others recognize Cate—which means neither of them has any trouble getting his—or her—fair share of waves.

"Your parents are so cool," Rae says to Luna as they watch Cate catch air. "My mother would rather die than get on a surfboard."

"Yeah, but your mother is an amazing horseback rider," Kanani points out. "My parents are so boring, it's unreal. Their idea of exercise is walking from one end of the mall to the other."

"So they're not athletes," Luna says. "They do other cool stuff. Your mom paints portraits, right? And your dad is a football fanatic."

"He watches it, but he doesn't play it," Kanani says. "In fact, he's a total couch potato."

"They adopted you and Cameron, right?" Luna says. "That's a cool way to start a family."

Kanani shrugs. She never really thought of it that way. She figured her parents adopted her brother and her because they couldn't have children of their own. What's so cool about that?

"I wonder what your birthparents are like," Rae muses.

"Pretty athletic, I'll bet, judging by Kanani," Luna declares.

"Maybe your dad is really some studly Hawaiian surfer dude," Rae suggests. "Someone famous, even. Wouldn't that be trippy?"

Kanani nods. She's often wondered about her birthparents. All she knows is that her father is Hawaiian and her mother is white—a *haole,* as the Hawaiians say. Everything else is a mystery—how they met, why they gave Kanani up for adoption, where they are now.

She's asked her adoptive parents a few questions over the years, but she hasn't gotten any useful answers. Mostly she gets the feeling her folks don't want to think about Kanani's and Cameron's lives before they were adopted. So she keeps her questions to herself. She doesn't want to hurt them, and really, what does it matter? They love her and she loves them. That's what counts.

"I'm starving," Rae says. "Let's go in and make lunch."

"I'm one step ahead of you," Luna's mom says, paddling over. "I made some sandwiches and left them in the cooler for you."

"Thanks, Mom," Luna says with a grin.

Kanani catches a wave. She makes it to the inside section, then it sucks out and pitches her into the sand. She staggers to her feet. She feels like she's been rolled in sandpaper!

A minute later, Luna and Rae join Kanani on the beach. "Did you see me eat it?" she asks with a laugh.

Luna nods. "It looked gnarly."

Kanani readjusts her bathing suit and a handful of tiny seashells fall out.

"Oh, man!" Rae exclaims. "I think you picked up half the beach."

"Now you know why we call it the Sandbox," someone drawls.

Kanani knows that voice. She turns and finds herself looking into the smiling face of the boy with the dimples. Now that she has a better look, she can see the rest of his face is just as attractive. His blond hair falls over his forehead and curls around his ears. His eyes are as blue as the Atlantic, and his smile is lopsided and teasing.

Back in elementary school, she decides, he was probably the kind of boy the girls chased across the playground and tried to kiss. She knows she would have given it a try.

"Thanks for helping me get that wave at the start of the session," she says. "It really upped our standing in the lineup."

"Yeah, the locals can get a little harsh sometimes. You know how it is. Every wanna-be surfer who comes to Florida tries to surf the inlet. Half of them don't know which way to point their board." He laughs. "Where you girls from?"

"Southern California," Luna says. "Crescent Cove."

"We're here to compete in the Longboard Open," Rae adds. "Luna and I are shortboarders, really, but we thought we'd give it a try. Kanani's the serious long-boarder."

"I could see that." He gives the girls a long, apprais-ing look. "So let me guess—you're triplets, right?"

The girls crack up. It's hard to imagine three girls who look more different—Luna with her tall, slender figure and streaky blond hair; petite Rae with her short strawberry locks; and Kanani with her toffee-colored skin and thick chestnut mane.

"Well, you're all so pretty," he drawls. "I was just haz-arding a guess."

Kanani rolls her eyes. "Oh, please."

"Don't mind me, I'm just jokin' around." He sticks out his hand. "My name is James Tibbets. J.T. to my friends. T-Bone to my enemies. Or is it the other way around? Well, for convenience's sake, you can just call me Darlin'."

"Or Loco." Kanani laughs, shaking his hand. "My name is Kanani."

"I'm Luna."

"Rae."

"Well, pleased to make your acquaintance. Anything you need to know about the area, just ask me. I've lived here all my life, and I've been surfing since I was six."

"Sorry to break this up," Rae says, "but can we eat now? My stomach is growling like a wild animal."

"Gotta go," Luna tells James. "She gets grumpy if you don't feed her regularly."

Kanani hesitates, wishing she could talk to James a little longer. He's got an aura about him, a charisma that burns like fire. She wants to stand a little closer and warm herself in the glow.

Luna and Rae start to walk away and Kanani reluctantly follows. But she hasn't gone two feet before she feels something touch her arm. She turns and there's James, smiling and motioning her closer. Curious, she waves Luna and Rae on and takes a step toward him.

"What?" she asks.

"Your name," he says. "What does it mean?"

" 'Pretty one,' " she answers shyly. "It's Hawaiian."

"And your eyes—are they Hawaiian too?"

"Half Hawaiian, half Caucasian."

"Which is which?" he asks with a smile. She giggles and he says, "I guess guys are always telling you how beautiful you are. It must get kind of boring."

Kanani shrugs. The truth is guys do flirt with her a lot. Her friends tell her it's because she's a knockout, but she doesn't see it. In fact, she feels like a freak with her sort of Asian eyes, her sort of Latina skin, her sort of Valley Girl voice.

James gazes at her intently. "A pretty face is nice, but I'm more interested in what's inside," he says. "And I can see there's plenty going on behind those eyes."

Kanani has heard a lot of pickup lines, but no one has ever said *that* to her before. She smiles, flattered and a little flustered.

James puts his hands on the hips of his board shorts. "Tell me, Kanani, who are you? I mean, what drives you? What are you passionate about?"

Kanani is speechless. Who *is* this guy? He's weird, but absolutely fascinating. "Well," she says at last, "I really care about the environment. This is the only world we've got, you know. It makes me sick to see how we're destroying it."

He nods thoughtfully. Then he asks, "What are you doing later tonight?"

"I—I don't know. Nothing special."

"Have you ever seen a sea turtle up close and personal?"

"I've never seen one, period," she says.

"Well, meet me by the concession stand at ten o'clock tonight. I'll take you on a moonlit walk you'll never forget."

Kanani frowns. Ten o'clock? No way Tuck and Cate are going to let her meet some local dude at ten o'clock at night. She should just say thanks but no thanks and tell James she'll see him in the surf tomorrow.

But there's something about him that makes her want to say yes. Those eyes, those dimples, that smile. The way he said, "I can see there's plenty going on behind those eyes." And what's this something special he's promising to show her? A wild sea turtle? She'd love to get a glimpse of one of those.

"Okay," a voice says, and she realizes it's her own.

He grins. "Ten o'clock by the concession stand. Don't be late." Then he turns and strolls off down the beach.

Later that evening, after another ripping surf session, Tuck cooks burgers and Cate makes a salad. They send Rae off to the market for sodas, and assign Luna and Kanani the job of setting the picnic table.

"What did you think of James?" Kanani asks as she unfolds the plastic tablecloth.

"Who?" Luna says blankly. "Oh, the guy on the beach. That's some accent he's got. I could barely understand him."

"I like it. He's cute too, don't you think?"

"I guess. Dimples don't do anything for me." She opens a box of plastic utensils. "Did I tell you David is driving down from Lakeland tomorrow?"

David is Luna's boyfriend. He lives in Florida, but she met him while he was visiting his grandparents in Crescent Cove at the beginning of the summer. In fact, Luna was his counselor at surf camp, and with her help, he overcame his fear of the ocean and learned to surf.

"That's great," Kanani says. She doesn't quite understand what Luna sees in David. He's handsome, yes, but moody and intense. To Kanani, he always seems vaguely annoyed about something. Still, she's happy for Luna. She's been totally bummed since David left Crescent Cove.

Kanani rips open a bag of chips and dumps them into a dish. Turning from the table, she spots Rae walking up the beach with the sodas. But she's not alone; James is walking with her.

Just the sight of him makes Kanani's heart leap into her throat. Then she notices that James and Rae are walking pretty close—almost touching, in fact. And they're talking, laughing, even leaning over to whisper in each other's ear.

Kanani feels a burning flash of some strange emotion shoot through her. *Get away from him,* she thinks angrily. And then she realizes she's jealous.

Get a grip, girl, she tells herself. *You have no claim on James. You barely know him.*

But her skin feels prickly and her stomach is churning. She sees James tickle Rae, sees her chase him up the beach and tickle him back.

Kanani turns away, her heart pounding. No boy has ever made her feel this way before. She's off balance and dizzy, like she's coming down with something.

What in the world is going on? she wonders. She's not the jealous type, never has been. But that angry feeling inside her just won't go away.

3

*L*ater that evening, Kanani is sitting at the picnic table, watching the stars and waiting impatiently for ten o'clock to roll around. She still hasn't figured out how she's going to slip away without Tuck and Cate noticing. All she knows is, one way or another, she's going. There's no way she's going to pass up a chance to see a wild sea turtle, or to spend time alone with James.

Rae appears out of the darkness and sits down beside her. "What's up?"

"Just looking at the night sky," Kanani replies.

"The moon looks close enough to touch."

Kanani nods, then says, "I saw you walking back from the store with James."

"Yeah, we just bumped into each other. Literally. He was buying a Yoo-hoo. Have you ever tried one of those?"

"It looks disgusting."

"That's what I thought. But J.T. gave me a sip and you know what? It's not bad."

"J.T.?"

"That's his nickname, remember?" Rae stretches out across the top of the picnic table and puts her hands behind her head. "He was telling me how to get a good launch off First Peak to catch maximum air. You can't do it on a longboard. J.T.'s a shortboarder, you know. And we found out we have something else in common. He plays the guitar."

Kanani scowls. She hates that Rae and James—J.T.—have discovered they have so much in common. And she hates that Rae seems so pleased about it.

For a moment, she considers telling Rae that James has invited *her* on a moonlit walk. Then she changes her mind. What if Rae tries to invite herself along? And what if James says okay? Kanani decides then and there to keep her mouth shut.

"I'm going to bed pretty soon," Rae announces. "When the sun comes up, I plan to be in the water, catching my first wave of the day."

Kanani checks her watch. Nine forty-five. Almost time to meet James. How is she going to slip away without getting into trouble?

A moment later, Luna's parents give her the answer. "Rae? Kanani?" Tuck calls, crawling out of their tent with Cate behind him. "You out here?"

"Over here," the girls call.

"We met some old friends out in the water today," Tuck says. "Bill and Suzie Corrigan. They invited us over to their campsite for a visit. You think you girls can take care of yourselves for an hour or so?"

"Sure," Rae replies. "I'm going to bed soon anyway."

"Luna's down at the showers," Cate says. "I think she's going to bed early too."

Kanani doesn't say a word about her plans, but no one seems to notice. When Tuck and Cate are out of sight, she turns to Rae and says, "I'm going to the store for a candy bar. You want anything?"

It feels weird to be lying to one of her best friends. Weird and kind of crummy. But she wants James all to herself.

"No, thanks," Rae replies.

"Okay. See you in a while." Kanani heads across the campground, walking faster and faster, until finally she breaks into a run. She arrives at the concession stand, sweating and out of breath. Oh, no, she can't let James see her like this! Quickly, she wipes her face with her sleeve and straightens her hair.

Her heartbeat is just starting to return to normal when she feels a pair of hands cover her eyes. "Guess who?"

"J.T.?"

He removes his hands and she whips around to face

him. But he's not smiling. "J.T.?" he says with a pout. "Don't use that silly nickname. I like it when you call me James."

"Hello, James," she says and smiles, secretly pleased to know he likes her name for him better than the one Rae uses.

His face lights up like a Christmas tree. "Ready for our walk?"

She nods and they stroll under the bridge to the Indian River Lagoon side of the north island. The sultry air envelops them like a steam bath, and the moon casts a silvery glow on the sand and the palm trees.

"Well, what do you think of Florida so far?" James asks.

"I like it. It looks a little like Hawaii. And the weather is tropical. That's like Hawaii too."

"I got plans to surf the North Shore someday," James drawls. "Do you go there a lot?"

Kanani sighs. "I wish. I left Hawaii when I was one month old and I've never been back."

"Well, if you get into competitive surfing, you'll have to go back. They hold a lot of important contests over there."

Why hadn't Kanani ever thought of that? It was so obvious. If she started winning longboard contests, she'd attract sponsors. If she had sponsors, they might send her to Hawaii to compete.

Suddenly, the Florida Longboard Open seems even more important, more serious—and more nerve-racking. Does she have what it takes to win a big contest like that?

She's thinking it over when she feels James reach for her hand. In a flash, her worries about the contest disappear. All that matters now is the feel of James's warm fingers entwined with hers. He leads her down to the water's edge and they walk slowly, not speaking. She can feel her heart beating against her ribs and hear the water lapping against the shore.

All at once James stops and puts his finger to his lips. "Look!" he whispers.

She follows his gaze, and her jaw drops. A sea turtle, almost three feet long, is slowly crawling out of the water. Its wet shell gleams in the moonlight. As Kanani and James watch, it moves slowly up the beach until it reaches the rolling sand dunes.

"Don't move," James whispers in her ear. "Even a tiny sound will scare her away."

The turtle sweeps the sand with its flippers, digging a hole.

"She's going to lay her eggs in that hole," James whispers. "They're huge—as big as Ping-Pong balls. Watch."

The turtle leans back into the hole, dropping her eggs. Then she covers them with sand and starts crawling again. But when she tries to turn back toward the water, her flipper catches in the low, creeping plants that grow over the dunes.

"She's stuck," Kanani whispers anxiously. "We have to help her."

James shakes his head. "Wait."

Kanani watches impatiently as the turtle continues to wag her flippers. Gradually, she breaks free of the foliage and resumes her slow crawl back to the sea. Finally, she reaches the water and disappears beneath the surface.

"Wow!" Kanani breathes. "That was amazing!"

"The eggs will hatch in a couple of months. That's a sight—hundreds of baby sea turtles crawling into the lagoon."

"Thank you for bringing me here, James. That was really special."

"You're pretty special yourself," he says with a grin.

Kanani gazes into James's blue eyes, her heart pounding. What is it about this guy that makes her feel so off balance?

Then she notices the moon, shining over his shoulder. It's higher in the sky than it was when they left the concession stand. "What time is it?" she asks with a worried frown.

"Oh, I don't know. Almost midnight, I reckon."

"Midnight! I have to get back. Tuck and Cate are going to kill me."

"Now don't you worry your pretty little head like that. I know a shortcut."

He takes her hand and they hurry back to the campground. When her campsite comes into view, she stops and whispers, "I better go the rest of the way alone."

"All right." She starts to leave, but he grabs her arm and spins her around. "Got a kiss for the boy who showed you your first Florida sea turtle?" he asks with a flirtatious smile.

Kanani's stomach does a back flip. She wants to kiss him—wants it with all her heart—but should she? She just met James this morning. She barely knows him. Finally, she stands on tiptoe and gives him a quick peck on the cheek. Before he can react, she turns and runs. "See you in the surf!" she calls over her shoulder.

He just stands there with his hands on his hips, grinning in the moonlight. "Good night, Kanani. Good night, Pretty One."

4

Kanani awakens with a smile on her face. She's remembering the feel of her hand cradled in James's hand, and his sweet face in the moonlight. Then she remembers how he asked her for a kiss, and a flush creeps over her skin that makes the Florida morning feel cool by comparison.

She unzips the top of her sleeping bag and marvels at her good luck. When she sneaked back into camp last night, Tuck and Cate were still out, and Luna and Rae were fast asleep. But she's lucky in other, much more significant ways too. She's three thousand miles from home on a magical adventure, exploring a tropical wonderland filled with sea turtles, osprey, and surf. Plus, for the first time in her fifteen years, there's a boy interested in Kanani who interests her too—one who cares about her not just for her pretty face, but for what's "going on behind those eyes."

"Luna?" says a voice outside the tent, and suddenly Luna leaps out of her sleeping bag, fully clothed.

"Wha—?" Kanani begins.

"It's David," Luna whispers. She unzips the flap of the tent and wiggles out—presumably into David's waiting arms.

Kanani grins. She understands exactly how Luna feels. Of course, she hasn't known James as long as Luna has known David. Still, she has a feeling her relationship with James is going to develop into something just as significant as Luna's love for David. At least she hopes it is.

Kanani rolls over to see if Rae is awake. All the jealousy she felt toward her friend last night has disappeared. In fact, in the bright light of day, it seems kind of silly. Rae isn't interested in James, Kanani knows that. She's got a boyfriend back in Crescent Cove, a lifeguard named Drew.

Well, Kanani decides, maybe Rae wouldn't call Drew her boyfriend, exactly, but they've dated a few times, and she seems to like him. Anyway, after last night's moonlit walk, Kanani is quite certain James isn't interested in anyone except her.

"Rae?" Kanani whispers, reaching out to shake her friend's shoulder. But the sleeping bag is empty.

Then Kanani remembers. Rae was planning to hit the surf early. She's probably out there now, practicing on one of the longboards Tuck brought along, preparing for the contest.

Kanani throws her arms over her head and stretches. Today is Monday; the contest isn't until Saturday. It was wise of Tuck and Cate to bring them to Florida early, Kanani decides. That way they have plenty of time to get used to the steamy Florida weather and the ripping Sebastian Inlet surf.

Kanani jumps up and roots among the piles of clothing on the floor of the tent until she finds her damp bathing suit. She slips it on, grabs her board, and makes a quick stop at the bathroom. Then she heads for the beach. First Peak is already crowded. She looks for James, but can't find him. She doesn't see Rae either. So she decides to head north and check out the other breaks.

Second Break and Third Break are pretty small, but OK Signs, the most northerly surf spot at the inlet, looks good. She paddles out and sits just outside the lineup, watching the waves roll in. It's only nine o'clock but already the sun feels hot on her shoulders.

A set wave is building and she's in the perfect position. She takes off, drops in, and cuts left. As the wave picks up speed, she walks to the nose and crouches there with the toes of her left foot dangling over the edge of the board. Then she walks back, drops down the wave, and cuts back hard, sending a rooster tail of spray shooting out behind her.

Oh, yeah!

Five waves later, Kanani sees Luna's dad paddling out. "Tuck," she calls, "hi!"

He paddles over. "I thought you'd be at First Peak, practicing for the contest."

"Later," she replies. "This morning I just felt like doing a little soul-surfing."

"I know what you mean." Tuck takes a wave and Kanani watches him with admiration. His style is so fluid, so effortless. He isn't trying to impress anyone, that's obvious. He's just waltzing with the wave, enjoying the dance.

Back in the lineup, Tuck pushes his shoulder-length gray hair off his face and remarks, "This place is alive with surf history."

"Really?" Kanani asks with interest.

"Matt Kechele perfected the first aerials at the inlet. Later, he became a mentor to another soon-to-be surf legend, Kelly Slater."

"Kelly Slater started here? Wow!"

"I used to travel out here once or twice a year," Tuck says. "This was back before Luna was born. Cricket's dad came with me once."

Kanani's eyes widen. Cricket, a member of her

Crescent Cove surf posse and one of her best friends, is the daughter of Chet "the Panther" Connolly. He's a legendary sixties surfer and a real wild card. These days he's practically a hermit, showing up in the surf when a big swell hits, then disappearing as soon as someone recognizes him. He's also a deadbeat dad, who walked out on Cricket and her mother ten years ago.

"You knew Chet Connolly?" Kanani asks.

"We were good friends once," Tuck says.

"Was he always so . . . I don't know—*weird?*"

Tuck smiles. "He was always a little different, that's for sure. He used to eat liverwurst and sardine sandwiches for lunch every day. He'd stick one in his wet suit and munch on it while out in the lineup. One time he decided to see what it felt like to surf naked—at Malibu Pier! Someone called the cops and he escaped by paddling straight out to sea and hitching a ride on a fishing boat!"

Kanani laughed. How wild would it be to have a dad like that instead of her ordinary, couch potato father? On the other hand, her dad is always there for her, while Cricket's dad is nowhere to be found. "Do you still keep in touch with him?" Kanani asks.

Tuck shakes his head. "When surfing started to get popular, Chet just couldn't take it. He hated the contests and the commercialism and the crowds. He started picking fights with the wanna-bes, letting the air out of their tires, things like that. He pulled it together for a while when Cricket was born—got a steady job, stayed out of trouble—but it didn't last long. One day he just took off, and I haven't seen him since."

"Wow," is all Kanani can say. Cricket's dad is a strange guy. She wonders if Cricket would be interested in Tuck's stories about her father back in the sixties. She decides to talk to Luna and Rae about it later.

Tuck and Kanani catch some more waves. Then Kanani heads in to eat some breakfast. Back at the campsite, she finds Rae kneeling beside the tent, waxing one of the longboards.

"Hi," Kanani calls, putting down her board. "Have you seen Luna and David?"

"David's here already?" she asks with surprise.

"He showed up around eight-thirty. Where were you?"

A smile creeps up Rae's cheeks. "I went kayaking with J.T."

Suddenly, Kanani doesn't feel hungry anymore. "What?"

If Rae notices that Kanani is upset, she doesn't let on. "He took me into the mangroves. What amazing trees they are! They grow right up out of the water, and the roots stick up into the air."

"No kidding," Kanani mutters, but what she's thinking is, *James took you kayaking? You, and not me?*

"We saw egrets and a heron. And, Kanani, just as we were leaving, I saw this big shadow in the water. We paddled closer and it was a manatee!"

A manatee! Kanani would kill to see one. They're rare—endangered, in fact—and Florida is one of the only places in the world where they live in the wild.

"It was huge," Rae continues. "J.T. says they grow to over ten feet long and one thousand pounds! And Kanani, they're so weird-looking. Like underwater elephants!"

"I know," Kanani says flatly.

Now Rae picks up on Kanani's unhappiness, but not the reason. "Maybe we can rent a tandem kayak and I'll take you back to the mangroves. J.T. told me he'd seen that manatee there before. Did you know you can identify them by the scars on their backs? J.T. said they get them from being hit by motorboats and—"

Kanani can't stand it anymore. "James and I went for a walk last night," she announces, a little too loudly. "We saw a sea turtle come out of the water to lay her eggs."

Rae stops talking and stares at Kanani. "James—I mean, J.T.—was with *you* last night?"

Kanani doesn't answer right away. Her skin is tingling and she feels sick inside. She's got to figure this out. Why would James ask Rae to go kayaking when he's so obviously interested in her?

Then, suddenly, she gets it. "What did you and

James talk about in the store?" she asks Rae. "Did you tell him you wanted to see a manatee?"

Rae looks at her blankly. "I didn't even know what a manatee was until J.T. told me. I guess I might have mentioned something about how cool it would be to see the mangroves. My father read an article about them and told me I should check them out when I was here. Why?"

Kanani nods knowingly. It all makes sense now. James asked Rae to go kayaking because she was curious about the mangroves and he wanted to help her out. That's totally different from his reason for asking Kanani to go walking with him. She hadn't said a word about wanting to see turtles. Nope, he'd asked her to meet him because he wanted to get to know her better. Because he had to find out what was going on behind her mysterious brown eyes.

Suddenly, Kanani isn't jealous anymore. In fact, she feels nothing but sympathy for Rae. "I have to ask you something, Rae," she says. "Do you like James?"

"Sure, I like him. What do you mean?"

"I mean, do you like him *that* way?"

Rae smiles a secret smile. "Kinda. Yeah."

Kanani bites her lips. "Rae, I'm sorry to have to tell you this, but James isn't interested in you. He likes me."

Rae's eyebrows lowered. "How do you know that?"

Kanani feels suddenly shy. She doesn't want to tell

Rae that James held her hand, or that he asked her for a kiss. That's special—just between them. "I just do," she replies, smiling her own secret smile.

"Really?" Rae asks coolly. "If James is hot for you, then why did he invite *me* to go jet-skiing with him tomorrow morning?"

Kanani feels like she's been slapped across the face. "Jet-skiing?" she asks, gulping. Inside, she's thinking, *James doesn't even like jet-skiing. He's into nature and preserving the environment, just like me.* But then she realizes she doesn't actually know that. She doesn't know much about James at all, except that he's charming and funny and cute, and she's crazy about him.

Rae looks worried. "I'm sorry, Kanani. I didn't mean to upset you."

Kanani isn't sure which she wants to do more—cry or scream. She pictures James and Rae paddling the kayak, laughing, talking—maybe even kissing. The thought sends an explosion of jealousy through her that burns like fire.

"Kanani?" Rae says anxiously. "I—"

But Kanani doesn't want to hear Rae's explanations or excuses. In fact, she doesn't want to talk to Rae at all. With hot tears in her eyes, she turns and walks quickly away.

5

The sun is just peeking over the horizon when Kanani takes off on her first wave of the day. The swell has gotten bigger overnight and now she's dropping into a barreling First Peak five-footer. But today her riding isn't a graceful dance with the wave. It's an assault. She rockets up the face, snaps off the lip, then charges into the barrel.

When the tube closes out, the white water slams her hard. It feels familiar—the physical version of the emotional hit she took when Rae told her James had asked her to go jet-skiing.

Kanani swims to the surface and laughs ruefully at herself. How like her to take this so seriously. *Get a grip, girl,* she tells herself. *So he doesn't love you. It's not the end of the world.*

But then why did it feel so special? When she was

standing with James in the moonlight, watching that sea turtle lay her eggs, Kanani felt as if she'd finally found her soul mate—someone who loved nature as much as she did, someone who really cared.

But no, James Tibbets is just as happy to go jet-skiing as he is to watch wildlife. What's more, he wants to do it with Rae. Intense, competitive, tomboyish Rae. Rae and Kanani are as different as day and night, black and white, shortboarders and longboarders. If James is attracted to Rae, surely he couldn't like Kanani.

There's that feeling welling up inside her again, that burning jealousy. She hates the way it ignites within her, destroying her equilibrium, overwhelming her good sense.

"Whoo-ee, that was a sweet ride!"

Kanani whips around and there's James paddling up behind her. Instantly, her heart takes off at a gallop. He's smiling at her—that sweet, dimpled smile—and her instinct is to smile back. But then she pictures him kayaking with Rae. Kanani's lips tighten into a thin line and she looks away.

"Excuse me, aren't you Kanani, the famous long-boarder from California?" James asks. "I know you're probably too busy to even talk to a nobody like me, but if I could have your autograph, miss, I sure would be grateful."

Kanani rolls her eyes. *What a flirt,* she tells herself. *He must practice these lines at home.*

"What's that?" he continues. "You don't have a pen? Well, that's no problem. For you I would swim to the bottom of the deepest ocean and squeeze the ink from an octopus. Then I would bring it back in an abalone shell and lay it at your feet."

"James, knock it off," Kanani mutters, trying not to let him get to her.

"What's wrong, California Pretty One?" He laughs with delight. "Cali Kanani—that's what I'll call you. It's the perfect nickname for you."

Cali Kanani. She loves the sound of it. But she won't let herself fall under his spell again. She can't. "I know you went kayaking with Rae yesterday," she says. "And the two of you are going jet-skiing this morning."

James looks bewildered. "Rae's your friend, right?"

"Yeah. So?"

"So don't you want me to be cordial to your friends? Rae said she wanted to see the mangroves, so I offered to take her. A quick tour in my buddy's tandem kayak. I thought you'd be pleased."

Kanani looks at him. "But you asked her to go jet-skiing with you too."

"That's right. She was asking about the jet skis and I mentioned that my buddy would lend me a couple of those too. She looked real excited, so I figured let's do it. You, me, Rae. It sounded fun."

"Me?" Kanani asks, bewildered.

"Well, of course you. I went to your campsite this morning to ask if you could come. I asked your friend Luna along too, but she's going surfing with her boyfriend. That's how I found out you were here— Luna told me."

Suddenly, it all makes sense. Rae has totally misread the situation. The realization makes Kanani wince. Rae is going to be so unhappy when she learns the truth— just as unhappy as Kanani felt when she thought the tables were turned.

"James," Kanani says anxiously, "I have to tell you something. Rae thinks you like her. I mean, she thinks this jet-ski ride is like . . . a date."

James looks alarmed. "Are you serious? Oh, wow. I feel terrible if I led her on. What should I do?"

"I guess you'll have to talk to her."

A pained look crosses his face. "Well, okay. But promise me you'll come jet-skiing. After what you told me, I don't want to spend any more time alone with her than I have to."

Kanani bites the inside of her cheek. Of course she has to come, but she doesn't feel good about it. "I don't like jet skis. They scare the wildlife and pollute the water," she says.

James shakes his head. "That's what I love about you. You're always thinking about the environment."

He looks toward the north jetty and sighs. "Truth is, I'd rather surf or kayak than tear up the water with a jet ski. But they *are* kind of fun, and if you only ride them out in the ocean, far away from the shore, I suppose they're not so bad." He shrugs. "Anyway, Rae looked so excited . . ."

Kanani considers. Actually, it might be fun. Interesting anyway. Besides, she isn't about to let James and Rae go alone—not a chance. "Okay, I'll come along."

James throws up his arms and lets out a whoop that sends him sliding sideways off his board. He hits the water with a splash. Then he swims over to Kanani's board and jumps on behind her.

"Hey!" she cries as he slips his arms around her waist.

He rests his head against her shoulder. "Now this is my idea of tandem surfing," he says.

She laughs. How could she have doubted James? He's just about the sweetest boy she's ever met. She grabs his wrists and wraps his arms even tighter around her waist. He kisses her ear and she lets out a sigh. She can hardly wait to go jet-skiing.

"Hi, James!" Kanani calls.

He's waiting on the dock for her, standing outside a wooden building with a sign that reads SEBASTIAN INLET

WATER SPORTS. "Cali Kanani," he says with a smile. "You ready to rock and roll?"

Kanani looks at the water vehicles lined up along the dock—kayaks, paddleboats, motorboats, jet skis. She wishes they were taking one of the sleek blue kayaks. Like Rae, she wants to paddle through the mangroves and see a manatee. But she's determined to be a good sport. "Let's do it," she replies with a nod.

Rae shows up a moment later, an eager smile on her pixieish face. But when she spots Kanani, her smile wilts. Ignoring Kanani, Rae turns to James and says, "But I thought—"

Before she can get out another word, James slips his arm around her shoulder and leads her down the dock. He leans close and speaks a few quiet words in Rae's ear—too quiet for Kanani to make out—and suddenly they're turning around and strolling back. Now Rae looks troubled and confused.

Kanani smiles sympathetically. Poor Rae. Kanani knows just how she feels. But before she can figure out what to say to make her friend feel better, a tall, muscular boy with short, black hair and nut brown skin walks out of the water sports shop and calls, "*Hola, T-Bone! Como estás?*"

"Hey, Francisco. Rae, Kanani, this is my friend Francisco. His uncle owns the water sports rental place. Our families have been friends since—I don't know— forever."

Francisco laughs. "Yes, about that long." He nudges James with his elbow and tells the girls, "Watch out for this one. He's trouble."

"Oh, thanks, buddy." James eyes the jet skis and rubs his hands together. "Let's get these babies fired up."

Francisco puts fuel in the jet skis. Then he hops on one of them and tools around beside the dock, shouting out instructions on how to start, stop, turn, and how to get on again if you fall off. "And believe me," he calls, "the first few times you ride one of these suckers, you *will* fall off."

Kanani glances at Rae. Her friend looks eager and confident. Kanani swallows hard. Motorized vehicles make her nervous. In fact, she's the only fifteen-year-old she knows who isn't dying to get her license. If it was up to her, she'd walk or ride her bike everywhere. And surf.

"Okay, enough talk," James says. "Let's hit the water." He hops on one of the jet skis and zooms around in a tight circle.

"Slow down, amigo," Francisco warns. "The speed limit is five miles an hour in the harbor—unless you want to pay another fine."

Another fine? Kanani wonders. But before she can ask about it, Francisco is helping her onto one of the jet skis. "Go on," he says, "give it a try."

Kanani nudges the accelerator and the jet ski jerks forward. It teeters left, then right, and finally tips over. Kanani hits the water with a shriek and a splash.

James laughs, then buzzes over and helps her back on. "Give it a little more gas," he advises. "You can't balance if you don't get some speed."

Behind her, Rae is climbing onto her jet ski. She takes off and putters around as if she was born riding the thing. Kanani stares at her enviously. Why is it so easy for Rae?

Kanani grits her teeth and tries again. After a few more tries—and a few more spectacular failures—she manages to steer the jet ski back and forth in front of the dock without tipping over.

"Okay," James calls, "we're ready to rip. Follow me!"

"Stay away from the shore and watch out for dolphins and manatees!" Francisco calls after them.

James revs his jet ski and takes off down the inlet in the direction of Indian River. Rae cruises behind him and Kanani brings up the rear, concentrating hard so she won't lose her balance. As they approach the lagoon, Rae maneuvers her jet ski until she's riding next to James. Kanani watches them chatting and laughing as they ride.

Once again, that familiar jealous feeling simmers inside her. She knows it's silly—James told her he wasn't interested in Rae—but she doesn't like being left out. She puts on some speed and manages to catch up to them.

Now they're riding side by side—Kanani to the left of James and Rae on his right. It's a tight squeeze, especially since Kanani and Rae don't always keep their jet skis going in a perfectly straight line. Kanani glances at James. His head is turning from side to side, like a spectator at a tennis match, and he looks a little worried.

Kanani knows she should probably drop back, but she just can't bear to leave Rae alone with James. She concentrates on keeping her jet ski moving at the same speed as James's jet ski, and parallel to his. Then suddenly, she looks up and sees a fishing boat on her left, looming frighteningly close.

Panicked, Kanani veers away from the boat—and right at James. His eyes grow wide. He hits the accelerator and roars ahead.

Kanani's heart is ricocheting against her ribs like a Super Ball. She slows down and tries to catch her breath. Meanwhile, Rae has zoomed ahead to keep up with James. She sees the two of them shouting something to each other—probably something about how totally lame Kanani is.

Relax, Kanani tells herself. *You can do this.*

She joins up with James and Rae. "Sorry about that," she says with an embarrassed smile.

James responds with his dimpled grin and Kanani's heart just melts. "Feel that wind?" he says, tilting his chin up. "There's a lot of good chop on the lagoon today. Let's have some fun."

He buzzes ahead with Kanani and Rae in the rear. Much to Kanani's relief, Rae doesn't even try to keep up with James this time. In less than a minute, they're far away from the shore, out in the windswept lagoon.

"Now let me show you what this baby can do!" James shouts.

He hits the accelerator hard and aims for a patch of choppy water. He roars up a wave, catches air, and touches down on the other side. Then he leans into a big turn, revs the engine, and does it again.

Kanani stares, astonished. If she could let go of the jet ski's handles, she'd applaud. Instead, she whoops her approval and shouts, "Way to go, James!"

Rae is whooping too, but then she adds, "I'm going to try it."

"Make sure you get enough speed," James calls. "Keep the jet ski steady, and when you land, don't slow down."

Kanani can't believe it. Rae is charging toward a patch of chop, gaining speed. Kanani tenses, preparing for Rae's painful wipeout. But to her total amazement, Rae hits the crest of the swell, lifts a few inches into the air, and lands it!

"Go, Rae!" James shouts. "You're a natural at this!"

Kanani knows she should be happy for Rae, but all she feels is irritation. Why is *she* getting James's attention and approval? *It should be me,* Kanani tells herself.

Kanani knows what she has to do. She has to catch

bigger air than Rae and she has to do it with more grace and style. *Okay*, she tells herself, *no problem.*

Before she can change her mind, she revs the accelerator and takes off, aiming her jet ski at a looming patch of rolling water. As she nears it, she realizes it's bigger than she thought, and her heart skitters like a frightened rabbit. But it's too late to turn back now. She launches off the crest and hangs there an instant.

The next thing she knows, she's falling sideways, gasping as she frantically tries to regain her balance. Her hands slip off the handles and flail helplessly. Then she hits the water hard, and everything goes black.

6

An instant later, Kanani's eyes flutter open. Instinctively, she kicks her feet and pops to the surface. But her head is spinning and she can't seem to catch her breath. She opens her mouth to call for help, but no sound comes out.

Suddenly, a hand tightens around her wrist and she feels herself being lifted out of the water. She gasps for breath and feels glorious, life-giving oxygen filling her lungs.

"You're going to be okay," a voice says. "You just had the wind knocked out of you."

Kanani's brain clicks into gear and she realizes the voice belongs to James. She looks around and sees she's sprawled across the back of his jet ski. Slowly, she sits up and pats her arms, her chest, her legs. Nothing broken, no major sprains or bruises. James is right. She's going to be okay.

"Are you all right, Kanani?" Rae calls. She's floating on her jet ski a few yards away, looking anxious.

Kanani nods. "I'm not sure what happened. I caught air, then the next thing I knew, I was underwater."

"You took off crooked and lost your balance," James explains. "Then your hand slipped off the accelerator, you lost speed, and oops—wipeout!"

Kanani manages a weak laugh. "I guess I'm not quite ready to pull off the big moves."

"Not today anyway," James replies. "You need to take a break. We're going in."

"You mean, back to the dock? Oh, no, I'm fine, really."

"Get real," Rae says. "You hit the water hard, Kanani. It hurt just to watch you."

She takes a deep breath. She has to admit her ribs are a little sore. "Okay, maybe you're right," she concedes.

It occurs to her that she can find her way back up the inlet by herself, that James and Rae can continue jet-skiing. But she doesn't want to leave James, and she definitely doesn't want Rae to be alone with him. So she lets him drive her to her jet ski and help her on it. Then the three of them ride back to the dock together.

When they get there, Kanani sees Francisco helping a

middle-aged couple into a tandem kayak. He hands the couple their paddles, then walks over to meet Kanani, James, and Rae.

"You're back early," he says with a puzzled frown.

"Kanani wiped out and got the wind knocked out of her," James explains. "I think she's had enough for one day."

"Yeah, but not me," Rae announces.

James turns to her. "You serious?"

"I had a blast out there," Rae says. "I can't wait to try it again."

Kanani tenses. What is Rae saying? Does she expect James to leave Kanani at the dock and go out again?

"How are you feeling, Kanani?" James asks.

She considers lying and telling him she's hurt. Anything to keep him from going off with Rae. But she's a terrible liar, and besides, she just can't believe James is going to leave her.

"I'm fine," she says. "A little sore, but it's no biggie."

James turns to his friend. "Francisco, keep an eye on Kanani, will you? Rae and I will be back in an hour, tops."

Kanani feels her jaw drop. He *is* leaving her. She watches in dismay as James and Rae cruise away from the dock, leaving her alone with Francisco. She wants to call them back. She wants to tell them she lied and she's really hurting. She wants to ask James why he's riding off with Rae when only a couple of hours ago he told Kanani he cared about her, only her.

But it's too late now. Besides, Francisco is holding out his hand to help her off the jet ski. She doesn't want to be rude, so she takes it and steps onto the dock.

"How about something to drink?" he asks.

Francisco is tall, probably six feet, and she realizes she'll have to look up to meet his eye. But she's afraid that if she looks at him, she'll start to cry. "No, thanks," she mutters, turning away.

"Okay. Well, uh, I'll be inside. If you want anything, just yell."

She doesn't answer. She knows she's acting weird, but she can't help it. She pictures James and Rae hopping waves and laughing at the memory of Kanani's pathetic wipeout. She pictures Rae flirting with James, giggling and batting her eyelashes. Never mind the fact that Rae has never batted her eyelashes at anyone in her entire life. Right now Kanani is so jealous, anything seems possible.

Francisco walks away and Kanani sits on the edge of the dock, shoulders slumped, staring down at the water. She doesn't know how long she's been sitting there when Francisco comes back and sits down beside her. He doesn't say anything, just hands her a bottle of water.

She opens the top and takes a sip. That's when she realizes how parched her throat is. She gulps the rest of the bottle and manages a small smile. "Thank you."

"No problem." He takes a swig of his 7UP. "You're from California, right?"

She nods.

"I was born in Cuba. My parents came here when I was two years old."

Kanani sits up a little straighter. "I was born in Hawaii. My mother took me to California when I was one month old."

He raises his eyebrows. "It seems we have something in common. Why did your mother leave Hawaii?"

"I'm not sure exactly. All I know is that she gave me up for adoption soon after she got to California. My adoptive parents lived in Crescent Cove. That's where I grew up."

Francisco nods thoughtfully. "My grandparents were political activists who fought against the Communists. Not long after Castro came to power, the government gave them one day's notice to pack their bags and get out."

Kanani bites her lip. "That must have been hard."

"Yes. Later, when I was born, my parents decided to follow my grandparents to the United States, but permission was denied. Eventually, they secured visas to Panama. We lived there for two years before we were able to join my grandparents here in Florida."

"And you never went back to Cuba?" Kanani asks.

Francisco shakes his head sadly. "If we did, we could be arrested. But someday, when Castro dies, I'll return.

It's not that I don't love this country," he adds quickly. "But Cuba is where my roots are."

"I know what you mean," Kanani says. "I love California, but Hawaii is my home. I won't be truly happy until I can go there again." She winces, suddenly aware of how stupid that sounds. "Sorry. I don't mean to be so melodramatic. My situation is nothing like yours. I mean, no one is going to arrest me if I go to Hawaii. I just don't have the money right now."

He smiles. "I understand. T-Bone says you're here to compete in the longboarding contest, right?"

She nods. "Do you surf?"

"A little. Not well enough to compete."

"I don't know if I'm good enough either. But I'm going to try." She pauses, thinking about what James told her. "If I win, one of the surf companies might decide to sponsor me. Then, next time there's a long-boarding contest in Hawaii, they'll pay my way."

"*Que bueno,*" Francisco says.

"What?"

"That's excellent."

Kanani laughs and glances at Francisco. Their eyes meet and she notices his are dark brown, like melted chocolate. She looks away, suddenly uncomfortable. She's talking to Francisco like they're old friends, telling him personal things she's barely discussed with her girlfriends.

Francisco is easy to talk to, and he seems sincerely interested in what she has to say. But is he just being polite? And why is she wasting her time talking about Hawaii when she could be asking him questions about James? Like he said earlier, their families have known each other for years. Francisco must have lots of interesting stories to tell, and she's dying to hear them.

Kanani is trying to think of a way to broach the subject when the growl of a jet ski catches her ear. She looks up and sees James and Rae riding toward the dock. The bow of James's jet ski looks brown and slimy, and there are a few strands of something that looks like grass stuck there.

Francisco jumps to his feet and motions James and Rae into an empty space beside the dock. Then he offers his hand and helps Rae off her jet ski.

"How'd it go?" he asks.

Kanani knows the answer. Rae's face is glowing with happiness. Kanani feels like shoving her into the water. Anything to wipe that infuriating smile off her face.

"We had a good time," James says. "Thanks for setting us up with the jet skis, man."

"It's cool," Francisco replies. "But tell me, T, you weren't riding in the mangroves by any chance, were you?"

"No way. We were hopping waves. Then we went around by the campground."

Kanani glances at Rae. She opens her mouth as if she's going to say something, then closes it again. She looks down at her feet.

Hmm, Kanani wonders, *what's going on?*

But before she can give it any more thought, James flashes his five-hundred-watt smile and says, "Gotta go. If I'm late for dinner, my mama will have my hide. I'll see you tomorrow in the surf, okay, girls?"

He jogs away, waving over his shoulder as he goes. Francisco walks over to help the middle-aged kayakers, who are paddling back to the dock. That leaves Kanani and Rae, standing alone in front of the shop.

Kanani looks at Rae uncertainly. They're supposed to be best friends, but somehow they've become rivals. It doesn't feel good, but Kanani doesn't know what to do about it. All she knows is that right now, the last person she wants to be around is Rae Perrault.

7

The next morning, the sky is gray, just like Kanani's mood. Luna and Rae are still asleep, and David's tent, which is pitched nearby, is tightly closed. Kanani steps out of her tent into the damp, muggy air and sighs heavily.

Where is James right now? she wonders. *Is he thinking about me like I'm thinking about him? Or is he daydreaming about Rae?*

The thought hurts more than her stiff muscles. She lies on her stomach and extends her arms, arching her back like a graceful cat.

"Kanani, have you seen the surf?" a voice calls.

It's Tuck, and he's jogging toward her with his board under his arm.

She scrambles to her feet and shakes her head.

"Wake up Luna and Rae," he tells her. "It's six feet and

building. There's a storm coming in—nothing serious, according to the locals I talked to, but it's going to produce some epic surf."

Kanani's pulse quickens. Sebastian's speedy barrels are exciting and challenging at four feet. At six feet, they'll be awesome!

Kanani steps into the tent and shakes Luna. "Rise and shine. The surf is cranking."

She leaves it to Luna to wake up Rae. She pulls on her bathing suit, hurries outside, and grabs her board. "You coming?" she asks Tuck.

"Gotta wake up Cate and grab something to eat," he replies. "We'll be there soon."

Kanani jogs to the beach. The sight of the surf makes her breath catch in her throat. It's gorgeous! She looks for James, but doesn't see him. Disappointment tugs at her, but the waves are so amazing that she can almost forget about how he hurt her yesterday—briefly, anyway.

Kanani throws her board in the water and charges into the crowded lineup. The best surfers are out today, and they're snagging the best waves. She waits patiently. Eventually, she catches the last of a six-wave set and roars down the line.

Whoa! The wave is so fast and so steep that it's all she can do to hang on. Finally, she pulls out just as a mountain of white water explodes beneath her.

Kanani lets out a whoop of joy and paddles back out. But when a half hour has passed and Luna and Rae still haven't shown up, she goes in to look for them. It's not like either of them to pass up surf like this. Is something wrong?

She walks up the beach. Second Peak is cranking, and Third Peak and OK Signs look good too. Maybe Luna and Rae decided to pass up crowded First Peak for another break.

She spots Luna's boyfriend, David, sitting on the beach at Third Peak. She waves and scans the water. Luna and Rae are out in the lineup, sitting side by side on two of Tuck's longboards. The sight makes her feel a little left out. Why didn't they look for her? And if they saw her out at First Peak, why didn't they wave her in and tell her they were planning to surf somewhere else?

After yesterday, she's not surprised that Rae doesn't want to surf with her. But what about Luna? It's not like her to forget about one of her friends.

"There you are!" Luna calls as Kanani paddles out to join them. "Where have you been?"

"At First Peak. What are you doing over here?"

"My dad said First Peak was really crowded, and Rae said you were planning to surf farther north."

"I didn't even talk to Rae this morning," Kanani says indignantly.

She glares at Rae, but Rae is getting into position to catch the next wave. Kanani can tell she isn't completely at ease on a longboard. Her paddling is slower than usual and she isn't in quite the right spot.

Kanani watches Rae take off. Without her shortboard, she can't make her usual tight cutbacks. She drops to the bottom of the wave and tries to snap up the face, but all she does is straighten out. The wave is breaking fast and a second later, the white water overtakes her. Kanani watches with satisfaction as Rae disappears into the soup.

Kanani takes the next wave. Rae is paddling out, and Kanani is sure Rae is watching her. It's mean, she knows, but she can't help showing off just a little. She pulls off a big bottom turn and crouches in the pocket. The wave closes out in front of her but she floats over the soup and drops into the inside section.

When the wave ends, Kanani paddles back out, a triumphant smile on her face. Rae doesn't look at her, but Luna slaps her a high five. "Sweet ride!" she exclaims.

"Thanks."

Kanani glances at Rae again. Rae runs her hands through her hair and shoots Kanani a self-satisfied smile. It's the smile of someone who has a secret, and Kanani wonders if Rae saw James this morning. Maybe he asked her to do something special with him this afternoon.

The thought makes Kanani's temperature rise. She takes a deep breath and reminds herself that James likes *her,* not Rae. If he's spending time with Rae, it's only because he doesn't want to be rude. Maybe she begged him to take her back to the mangroves to look for the manatee—something like that.

Still, Rae's smile is nagging at Kanani, making her worried. Rae has the hots for James—that's no secret. She wonders if something happened yesterday afternoon when they were jet-skiing. Maybe Rae told James something bad about Kanani—a lie that would make him stop liking her and start liking Rae instead.

Now Kanani's blood is boiling. She sees Luna take off. Then she notices Rae paddling awkwardly for the next wave. Suddenly, it occurs to Kanani, *I could beat Rae to that wave.*

Before she can change her mind, Kanani paddles around Rae and drops in front of her.

"Hey!" Rae shouts, but Kanani ignores her. She carves up the wave, straightens out, walks to the nose. As the board starts to dip, she walks back, turns hard, and pulls out. A beautiful ride.

Paddling out, Kanani sees Rae taking off on another wave. She surfs past Kanani, carving hard. Spray flies into Kanani's face.

Out in the lineup, Luna is waiting for Kanani with a bewildered frown. "What was that all about?"

"What?"

"What do you mean *what*? You snaked Rae's wave."

Kanani shrugs. "She wouldn't have gotten it. Her paddling isn't strong enough."

Luna stares. "But snaking her wave? Come on, Kanani, that's not like you. What's up?"

Kanani feels a stab of guilt. Luna is right. It's not like her. But today she feels justified. Rae is always so intense and competitive, so totally aggro. Kanani is just giving her a taste of her own medicine.

Rae paddles back out and glowers at her.

"I'm just trying to be more like Rae," Kanani announces. She glances at Rae. "That's how they surf on the pro tour, right?"

Rae doesn't answer. Instead, she turns and takes off on another wave.

Luna looks stunned. "What's with you two? Ever since we got here, you've both been acting weird."

"You know that boy we met the first day? James Tibbets? He likes me—he told me so—and I like him too. But Rae's decided she wants him for herself. She's been flirting with him, asking him to take her kayaking—as if Rae was into kayaking!—doing everything she can think of to make him forget about me."

Kanani realizes her voice has been getting louder and higher with every sentence. She falls silent, feeling foolish.

"I thought Rae was seeing that lifeguard who owns Barrels—I mean, Barney," Luna says.

Barney is a dog that Luna, Kanani, Rae, Isobel, and Cricket found on the beach earlier in the summer. They named him Barrels and cared for him until they found his owner, a lifeguard from Sola Beach named Drew.

"That's what I'm saying," Kanani declares, her voice growing harsh again. "Rae has more boyfriends than she knows what to do with. First she was seeing Shane Fox. Then she started going out with Drew. But I guess that isn't enough for her. She wants James too."

Kanani bites her lip. She doesn't usually lose her temper like this. The only time she even raises her voice is when she's working to save the environment. Like earlier in the summer when she was trying to find out what was causing the pollution in Owl Canyon Creek. Luna called her the Hawaiian Hurricane because she threw herself into the investigation with the force of a tropical storm.

But getting so worked up over a boy? This is something new, and she doesn't quite understand it.

It seems Luna doesn't either. "I don't think you should come down so hard on Rae," she says. "I mean, you're the gorgeous one, the one who always has boys trailing after her. Rae never had a boyfriend until this summer."

"I'm not gorgeous," Kanani protests. "Anyway, I don't want boys going after me because of the way I look. That's so shallow. James likes me because of who I am, not what I look like."

"Really?" Luna says skeptically. "He seems like a big flirt to me."

Kanani can't believe what she's hearing. Okay, sure, James likes to joke and tease. But so what? Luna is talking like he's some kind of James Bond playboy.

"That is so not true!" she retorts. "Anyway, what do you know? Your idea of a great guy is Mr. Deep and Moody David. Dating him is like dating an undertaker!"

Luna looks as if she's been punched in the solar plexus. "If this is what falling in love does to you," she says evenly, "I hope it's over soon. You need an attitude adjustment."

Now it's Kanani who feels stunned. She thought Luna was her friend! But now . . . well, she just isn't sure.

Luna catches the next wave and rides it in. David is waiting for her with a smile and a hug. Rae paddles in a moment later. The three of them disappear up the beach together.

Kanani stares after them in disbelief. Her two best friends have just left her without a word of good-bye. Suddenly, she wishes she hadn't snaked Rae's wave, hadn't gone out of her way to show off. Most of all, she wishes she hadn't bad-mouthed Luna's boyfriend.

Kanani catches another wave, but the thrill is gone. She paddles in and follows her friends' footprints up the beach, feeling lonely and all alone.

8

Kanani awakens the next morning to the sound of rain beating against the tent. She sits up and rubs her eyes. The wind is blowing and the sky is dark. The air is so damp and heavy that it seems to be pressing in on her. With a groan, she rolls over and pulls the sleeping bag over her head.

Rae wakes up a minute later. "Bummer," she mutters.

Kanani hears her getting up. Is she sneaking off to meet James? "You're going out in this?" Kanani asks.

"Yeah," Rae mutters. "Unless you want me to go to the bathroom right here."

"Oh," Kanani mumbles, feeling foolish.

Luna sits up. "Wait for me, Rae." She rummages in her backpack and pulls out a raincoat.

Rae puts on her raincoat too, and Kanani realizes

with a sinking feeling that she didn't pack one. What was she thinking? Tuck and Cate had told her she might need one.

She's too embarrassed to admit her mistake, so she just sits there, listening to Luna and Rae laughing and shrieking as they run to the bathrooms. A few minutes later, she hears them come back and climb into Tuck and Cate's tent. Now Kanani gets up and makes her own bathroom run. By the time she returns, she's dripping wet.

Kanani hears someone climbing out of Tuck and Cate's tent. She peeks out the flap. Luna is carrying a carton of orange juice and some breakfast bars. Kanani's stomach rumbles expectantly. But instead of coming back to her tent, Luna runs to David's tent and calls, "Are you awake?"

"Come on in," he answers, and she does.

Kanani knows that if she wants something to eat, she'll have to go into Tuck and Cate's tent. But Rae is there. Kanani sits on her sleeping bag, fuming. Why does Rae have to be such a pain? She can find her own boyfriend. Why is she trying to snake Kanani's?

Finally, hunger wins out and Kanani runs to Tuck and Cate's tent. "Morning, Kanani," Tuck says as she climbs in.

"We've got cereal and milk, OJ and breakfast bars," Cate adds.

"And rain. Lots of rain," Tuck chuckles.

"A breakfast bar will be fine, thanks," Kanani says.

Rae says nothing, just munches her cereal.

"Remember I told you the locals thought this storm wasn't going to amount to much?" Tuck says. "Well, they were wrong. I talked to one of the park rangers this morning and he says what we've got here is a tropical depression."

"What's that?" Kanani asks.

"A storm with winds less than thirty-nine miles per hour," Tuck explains. "With luck, it won't develop into anything more."

"What do you mean, 'anything more'?" Rae asks, looking up.

"A storm with winds over thirty-nine miles per hour is called a tropical storm," Tuck says.

"Over seventy-four miles per hour and you've got a hurricane," Cate adds.

"A hurricane!" Kanani cries.

"The ranger doesn't think that's going to happen," Tuck says quickly.

"Hurricane surf is supposed to be awesome!" Rae exclaims.

"Totally," Cate agrees.

Kanani bites the inside of her cheek. She's seen photos of hurricane surf that make the North Shore look like a bathtub.

"Can we surf today?" Rae asks eagerly.

"We'll check it out, definitely," Tuck replies.

Kanani isn't sure she wants to surf in the wind and the rain. But if James is out there—well, that's a different story.

They finish eating, and Cate goes to get Luna and David. Everyone except David—a beginning surfer who isn't up to charging big waves—changes into their bathing suits and grabs their boards.

At First Peak, Kanani stops and stares. The surf is six to eight feet and ripping, and the lineup is crowded with hot surfers. She looks for James, but doesn't see him. She tries not to care—after all, last time she saw him, he left her on the dock and went off with Rae. Still, she knows the sight of his shaggy hair and lopsided grin would turn the rain into a rainbow.

"It's like surfing in the shower," David declares, gazing out at the rain-spattered waves.

"Well, then, let's go wash off," Tuck says with a grin.

Cate paddles out at First Peak, but Tuck takes the girls to the less crowded but still cranking Second Peak. The current is strong and Kanani has to paddle hard just to stay in the lineup. It's not really her kind of surf. She prefers warm sunshine on her shoulders and a mellow vibe. This is rain in your face and grinding tubes.

Still, if she wants to win the contest, she knows she

has to be prepared to surf in any condition. And right now, the conditions at Second Peak are wild and woolly. So she forces herself to take off on wave after grinding wave, until her bathing suit is filled with sand and her arms feel like overcooked spaghetti.

"I never surfed waves that big before without wearing a wet suit," Luna exclaims. "It felt great!"

The girls are sitting in David's tent, eating Clif Bars and gulping Gatorade.

"You got some epic rides," David says, putting his arm around her waist. He pretends to shiver. "Just the thought of paddling out into waves like that makes my hair stand on end."

"Hmm, that might look good," Luna jokes, thrusting her fingers into his curly locks and lifting them up.

"Did you see my last wave?" Rae asks. "I caught massive air."

Kanani looks away. Ever since Rae came in second at the Western Championship, all she does is brag about her surfing.

"I mean, it was huge!" Rae declares.

"That nosedive you did at the end was pretty impressive too," Kanani can't resist saying.

Rae stares at her. "At least I go for it," she retorts. "You were surfing like an old lady."

Rae's words cut deep because Kanani suspects there's some truth in them. But she isn't about to admit it. "Just wait until the contest," she shoots back. "Then we'll see who has the best longboard style."

The tension in the tent is so thick you could spackle a wall with it, so when Cate sticks her head through the flap a moment later and asks, "Monopoly anyone?" they all cry, "Yes!" in unison.

Cate sits down and sets up the game. Immediately, Rae begins buying property and putting up houses. When she runs out of money, she convinces David to lend her some.

Typical, Kanani thinks. *She wants everything, even what isn't hers.*

Kanani only buys the property that appeals to her. Virginia Avenue and States Avenue because she likes their violet color; the railroads because her little brother Cameron is a model-train fanatic.

By the third time around the board, everyone is paying rent to Rae. Then, the fourth time Luna passes Go, her luck turns bad. First, she has to pay Income Tax, then Luxury Tax; then she ends up in jail and is forced to pay two hundred dollars to get out. Finally, she lands on one of Rae's most expensive properties: Park Place with a hotel.

"I can't pay," Luna groans, tossing down her miniature thimble. "I have to declare bankruptcy."

"Bad luck," David says sympathetically.

Rae looks at her thoughtfully. "Maybe we can strike a deal."

"A deal?" Luna asks, eyes widening. "Like what?"

"You give me all your property, and I'll make you my partner. You'll get twenty-five percent of everything I earn."

"Sweet," Luna says.

"Unfair!" Kanani exclaims.

Rae frowns at her. "It is not."

"Is too. Once you're bankrupt, you're out of the game. It says so in the rules."

"Prove it," Rae snaps.

"We can't," Cate interrupts. "We lost the sheet with the rules years ago. We rely on memory."

"Or make them up as we go along," Luna chuckles.

"Then Luna and I can cut a deal," Rae announces.

"Why not?" Luna says.

Kanani scowls. Rae is just too annoying to believe. And now she's got Luna going along with her. "The rules are the rules, even if we don't have them in front of us," Kanani insists. "Anyway, I remember what they say. If you're bankrupt, you're out of the game."

"Oh, come on," Rae gripes. "That's the ten-year-old version. This is the way they play in the real world."

"Long live capitalism!" Luna proclaims.

Everyone laughs—except Kanani. "That's the way *you* play maybe," she says, glowering at Rae. "But let me tell you something, girlfriend. You won't win."

Rae looks at her blankly. Then something clicks. "Oh, I get it. This isn't about Monopoly, is it? It's about J.T."

Kanani knows deep down that Rae is right. But she isn't about to admit it. "I don't know what you're talking about. I just don't like playing games with people who cheat and—"

"Okay, that's enough," Cate breaks in. "This game is over." She closes the game board. "I think the rain is making us all a little edgy. Who wants to go to the mall?"

All heads turn her way. "There's a mall near here?" Luna asks eagerly.

"I don't care if it's on the other side of the state," Cate replies. "I'm going to find it."

"I think there's one in Vero Beach," David says.

"Close enough." Cate nods. "Everybody get cracking. The Cate Martin Mall Express leaves in five minutes."

Kanani jumps up gratefully. She can't believe she lost her temper like that. What's happening to her? She feels so embarrassed she'd like to dig a hole in the sand and crawl into it.

David has returned to his own tent, and Rae is changing into a white blouse with dark red flowers embroidered around the open neck. Kanani considers. Maybe she should apologize. Rae did bend the rules a little, but who cares? It's just a game, right?

But at that moment, Rae notices Kanani looking at her. "J.T. told me he likes this blouse," she says, running her fingers through her hair. "Who knows? Maybe we'll run into him at the mall."

Kanani changes her mind so fast she can feel her brain cells sizzling. She can let it slide when Rae bends the rules of Monopoly. But bending the rules of love is unforgivable.

With an angry snort, Kanani pulls off the T-shirt and shorts she was planning to wear and slips into a miniskirt and a short pink blouse. She looks hot— hotter than Rae—and she knows it.

"Maybe we *will* run into James," she says. "In fact, I hope we do. Then we'll see whose outfit he likes best."

Kanani watches Rae's face crumple. For an instant, she feels sorry for her friend. Then an image flashes through her mind—James and Rae, riding off on their jet skis together. Kanani's heart hardens. Before she can change her mind again, she stands up and climbs out of the tent.

9

"Okay, we'll meet back here at four o'clock," Cate says. "Take a look around so you remember the spot."

Kanani looks up at the escalators and down at the benches and plants. Nearby, a vendor is selling watches and sunglasses from a cart.

"Have fun, kids," Tuck says. He takes Cate's hand and they walk toward the bookstore.

"Later," David calls. He and Luna stroll in the opposite direction, toward the skate and surf shop.

Kanani and Rae glance at each other uneasily.

It's so weird, Kanani thinks. *Just a few days ago, we'd be cruising the mall together, boy-watching and window-shopping. But now . . .*

Rae turns abruptly on her heels and strides to the escalator. Kanani is left alone, wondering which way to go. Finally, she wanders over to the mall directory and reads the listings. But without her friends to hang with, nothing in the mall seems very interesting right now.

Kanani's mind drifts back to Crescent Cove. What are Isobel and Cricket doing right now? Surfing at Paintball Point? Laughing and talking over blended mochas at Java Jones? Kanani was sad at first since neither Cricket nor Isobel was able to join them on the trip because of prior commitments at home. But now she wishes she was there with them. In fact, right now even her couch-potato family sounds pretty appealing. She wouldn't mind baking some peanut butter cookies with Mom, or even watching a football game with Dad and Cameron. But they're three thousand miles away.

Kanani walks listlessly past the chain stores and fast-food restaurants. How eagerly she'd anticipated this trip! Sunny skies, fun waves, a chance to spend time with two of her best friends—that's how she'd pictured it. And now . . . well, it seems nothing has turned out the way she expected. The sunny skies have turned to rain clouds, the fun waves have become bone-crushing slammers, and her best bud is trying to snag the only boy she's ever wanted.

And the infuriating thing, she tells herself, *is that I'm the one James smiled at first, the one he talked to and complimented and invited for a walk.*

So why is Rae going after him like he was the last boy on earth? And why is he responding like a kitten chasing a string?

Kanani walks aimlessly into the nearest shop—an accessories store called Bangles. She gazes at the hair clips, the purses, the jewelry. But her mind keeps bouncing back to James.

Why do I want him so much? she wonders. She's never let a boy get to her like this before. But there's something about James that sends her brain spinning like a merry-go-round. Those sparkling blue eyes, those dimples, that sweet Southern accent—she feels mushy-kneed just thinking about him. And then there's his charm, his goofy sense of humor, and the way he looks at her like she's the only girl in the whole wide world.

A feeling of longing gnaws at Kanani like an insatiable hunger. She turns from the mirror and hurries out of the store before anyone notices the tears welling up in her eyes. She's walking fast now, trying to get away from the confused feelings that are haunting her.

Up ahead, she sees another group of benches. Nearby, there's a table with a sign that reads SEBASTIAN INLET PRESERVATION COALITION. Eager to forget her troubles, she walks closer and studies the displays that cover the table.

The coalition, she learns, is a group of water-sport enthusiasts and environmentalists who have joined together to promote safe use of the inlet. With growing interest, Kanani reads the displays about the land and sea animals that inhabit the inlet, and what hikers, boaters, and jet-skiers can do to protect them. Inside her, a burning flame of passion is rising. If she lived here, she would do everything she could to protect the inlet. If she lived here, she would join the coalition and—

"Care to give a donation, miss?"

Kanani turns around and finds herself looking into the smiling face of James's friend Francisco. He's carrying a stack of pamphlets and a jar filled with coins and dollar bills.

"Hi!" she exclaims. "Do you volunteer for the coalition?"

He nods. "What about you? You interested in all this tree-hugger stuff?"

"You better believe it. If people don't learn to live in harmony with nature, there won't be any more nature—or any more people either."

"I guess we think alike," he says.

"But your family rents jet skis and powerboats," Kanani responds. "How does that help the environment?"

Francisco shakes his head. "Boy, you don't mince words, do you?"

Kanani winces, afraid she's offended him, but he just chuckles and says, "First of all, just because my uncle makes his living renting jet skis doesn't mean they're *my* favorite mode of transportation. I mean, who do you think convinced him to rent the kayaks? Furthermore, I believe there's room for everyone in the inlet as long as we all behave responsibly."

Francisco's speech puts Kanani in instant Hawaiian Hurricane mode. "But what about the manatees? I read that almost every one of them is scarred from being hit by a motorboat. And then there are the dolphins. Did you know that—"

"Kanani, are you busy right now?" Francisco interrupts.

His question brings her up short. "Well . . . no," she says at last. "My friends and I just came to the mall to kill some time until the rain stops. Why?"

"How about walking with me and helping me collect donations for the coalition? We can talk while we work."

She looks up into his dark chocolate eyes. They're deep and thoughtful—a bit like the eyes of Luna's boyfriend, David, except not so moody and ultraserious. She finds herself smiling. "Sure. Let's go."

They walk through the mall, handing out pamphlets and soliciting donations. "Check this out," Francisco tells her when the crowds thin out. He hands her a pamphlet with the title "Boaters and Manatees—Can They Share the Inlet?"

"The answer is yes," he says. "The boaters just have

to learn to behave responsibly. That means sticking to the deep channels, avoiding the shoreline and the sea-grass beds, wearing polarized sunglasses so you can watch for manatees in the water—stuff like that."

"The same goes for jet-skiers?" she asks.

"Absolutely. You just have to stay away from the shoreline, and don't go bombing around like a maniac."

"I thought that was the whole point," Kanani says with a wry smile.

Francisco laughs. "There are some loose cannons out there, for sure. But jet-skiing can be a blast. I mean, come on! Didn't you enjoy your ride the other day?"

"It was exciting," she admits, "but a little scary. When I hopped that wave, I felt totally out of control."

"I blame T-Bone for that. He should have taken things a lot slower. You don't charge big chop your first time out. That's wack."

"It's not James's fault," Kanani says quickly. "He was just trying to show us a good time."

"By bombing ahead and showing off, then encouraging you and your friend to do the same?" Francisco shakes his head. "That's not my idea of a good time. You could have been seriously hurt."

Kanani frowns. Is Francisco implying that James is an irresponsible jet-skier? The kind who breaks the rules and endangers the wildlife? No, she can't believe it. James cares about the environment. He'd never do anything that might hurt an animal.

"It was my idea to charge that wave," she says. "If you're going to blame anyone, blame me."

"If you say so," Francisco replies. "But next time you go jet-skiing, go with me, okay? We'll take it slow and easy and I guarantee you'll have a good time."

"All right," she agrees.

They walk on, handing out pamphlets and collecting donations. After a well-dressed woman stuffs a twenty-dollar bill in the jar, Francisco says, "I think we can take a break for a while." He nods toward a sandwich shop called La Playa Azul. "Have you ever had a Cuban sandwich?"

"No, what's that?"

"Try one. My treat."

Francisco walks up to the window and orders in Spanish. Soon the waitress is handing him two sodas and two delicious-smelling sandwiches on thick, fried bread. Kanani's stomach growls loudly.

"See, I knew you were hungry," Francisco says with a laugh.

They sit down on a nearby bench. Kanani takes a bite. "Wow! What's in it?" she asks.

"Ham, pork loin, cheese, pickles," he replies. "The real secret is the Cuban bread. They grill it in a *plancha*— a special grill, kind of like a clothing iron. *Es delicioso, verdad?*"

"What?"

"It's delicious, isn't it?"

"Oh!" she says and laughs. "Yes!"

He stretches out his long legs and asks, "So how's your vacation going? Are you enjoying our sunny Florida weather?"

Kanani giggles, then shrugs. "It started fine, but now . . ." She thinks of James and her heart aches, but she's not about to tell Francisco that. Instead, she says, "I always tell people I'm going to surf the North Shore of Hawaii one day. But I think I have to face the truth. I'm not ready for waves like that. I mean, this morning at the inlet, the surf was grinding. I should have charged it but . . ." Her voice trails off and she looks away.

"Why are you punishing yourself, Kanani?" he asks. "There's no wrong or right in surfing. All that matters is what feels good to you."

"But if I'm going to win the Florida Open, I have to be able to surf what's out there, and surf it better than anyone else. I'll never land a sponsor if I wimp out. They'll never send me to Hawaii!"

"Hold on," Francisco protests. "You're putting all the power in someone else's hands. There are other ways to get back to your island. Apply for a job, win a college scholarship. If you want it bad enough, you'll find a way. Maybe not today, maybe not tomorrow, but someday."

Kanani looks at Francisco. He seems so sure of himself, so confident. He knows who he is, and he isn't about to change to suit someone else. "I wish I could be like you," she says. "I mean, my friends think I'm this totally together person. But inside, I don't feel that way at all. Who am I? Where do I belong? What do I want? I'm just not sure."

Kanani looks away, shocked that she has revealed her deepest fears to a boy she hardly knows. But Francisco doesn't seem the least bit alarmed. He touches her chin and turns her toward him. "I'm not as confident as you might think. But *mi abuela*—my grandmother—says everyone must look deep inside, past the layers of fear and confusion, to find *la alma de la luz*—the shining soul—which is the true you."

"*La alma de la luz,*" she repeats. "I like the sound of that."

"When you discover it, you'll be beautiful—not just on the outside as you are now, but on the inside as well."

Kanani thinks back to that first day on the beach when James told her he was interested in what was going on behind her eyes. His words made her tremble inside. But when Francisco speaks of the beauty inside her, Kanani doesn't fall apart. Instead, she feels calm and centered and hopeful.

"Check it out," Francisco says, pointing toward a crowd of people who are streaming out of the nearby movie theaters. "Let's go spread the word about the coalition."

Kanani and Francisco throw away their trash and pick up the pamphlets and the donation jar. Together, they walk toward the crowd. Then, suddenly, Kanani catches a glimpse of a familiar strawberry-blonde.

"Hey, look," Francisco says. "Isn't that T-Bone and your friend?"

James and Rae are walking out of the theater, hand in hand. Kanani stops short. Her stomach sinks like a boulder rolling off a cliff. They're coming closer, talking and laughing. Any second now, they'll see her. But she can't face them—she just can't. Thrusting the pamphlets into Francisco's hands, Kanani turns and runs.

10

"Wake up, girls! I've got important news!"

It's Cate, calling from outside the tent. Her voice is barely audible above the howling wind.

Kanani pulls the sleeping bag over her head. She doesn't want to wake up—not if it means facing the fact that James and Rae are a couple. It just hurts too much.

But Cate unzips the tent flap and climbs inside. "The tropical depression has been upgraded to a tropical storm," she says. "The contest has been postponed."

Suddenly, Kanani is wide awake. "Until when?" she asks, sitting up.

Cate shrugs. "There's no telling. But it looks like we're going to miss it."

Kanani feels like crying. There goes her chance of winning the Florida Longboard Open, as well as her chance of landing a sponsor who will pay her way to Hawaii.

Luna lets out a groan and props herself up on one elbow. "This trip isn't turning out the way I pictured it."

"That's for sure," Rae says, sitting up. "But at least you've been able to spend time with David."

"You've had some fun too, I think," Luna says, playfully punching her friend's arm.

Rae laughs and rolls away. Kanani keeps silent, but inside she's thinking, *If stealing my boyfriend is your idea of fun, I'm glad we're not friends anymore.*

"Tuck called the airlines and tried to change our tickets so we could go home today," Cate explains. "But I guess everyone else is trying to do the same thing. There aren't any seats available."

"So we're stuck here?" Kanani asks miserably.

"Well, it's not *that* bad," Cate replies with a smile. "The waves are all-time."

"Bigger than yesterday?" Rae asks eagerly.

"Eight to ten feet. And the good news is it's not raining, at least for the moment."

"I want to surf!" Rae exclaims, throwing off her sleeping bag.

"Me too!" Luna agrees.

Kanani hesitates. She didn't feel comfortable in yesterday's surf. Can she handle what's out there today? Does she even want to try?

"I'm going out," Cate says, "and anyone who wants to come is welcome. We'll stick together and I'll keep an eye on you. But if you have any hesitation at all, don't go. This is serious tropical storm surf, girls. I mean *serious.*"

Cate leaves, and Luna and Rae run to the bathroom. Kanani lies there listening to the wind howl. Where is James right now? she wonders. Is he lying in his bed, dreaming of Rae?

The thought cuts her like a razor blade. Oh, why did Rae have to come on this trip? She's not a longboarder, and she certainly doesn't care about winning a longboarding contest. If she'd stayed back in California, Kanani and James would be together right now.

A figure appears outside the tent. "Hello in there! I'm looking for Luna."

"She went to the restroom."

David squints through the tent flap. "Oh, hi, Kanani. You going surfing today?"

"I don't know. Luna and Rae are going out for sure."

David shakes his head. "That girl of mine is a total go-getter!" He grins. "Guess that's why I adore her."

He runs back to Tuck and Cate's tent, leaving Kanani to ponder his words. How casually he threw out the phrase "that girl of mine." Luna is his and he knows it. No doubts, no worries.

Kanani longs to hear James call her "that girl of mine,"

and to know it's true. She imagines him telling his friends about Kanani's accomplishments, and exclaiming, "I guess that's why I adore her!"

But it's just a fantasy, she knows that. James belongs to Rae now.

Luna and Rae return. They throw off their pajamas and slither into their bathing suits.

"You coming, Kanani?" Luna asks.

"I—I don't know."

"Why don't you just come down to the beach and check it out?" Luna suggests.

Rae says nothing. She's not even looking at Kanani. *She feels guilty,* Kanani thinks. *She knows she poached my guy.*

"Okay, sure," Kanani says. She puts on her bathing suit, followed by sweatpants and a hooded sweatshirt.

The whole crew heads for the jetties—Tuck, Cate, David, and the girls. They walk slowly, fighting the wind. The palm trees are bending low and sand is blowing everywhere. Empty soda cans rattle across the parking lot.

"The lineup isn't even that crowded," David remarks.

Quickly, Kanani searches the waves for James. She's not sure if she wants to see him or not. But he's not there.

"Only the big boys are out today," Tuck says.

"And the big girls," Rae adds, waxing down her board.

Check out your Luna Bay
Lovescope and Surfscope!

Luna is always trying to find out when to catch the best waves—but surf reports aren't the only kind of forecasts she likes. She also loves to check out her good friend Natalie's column in the local *Crescent Cove Reporter*, featuring the best love- and surfscopes. Take a look below and see what's in store for you!

LEO July 23–Aug. 22 *LOVESCOPE* If you've ever wanted to change your look, now would be an opportune time. An adventurous new hairstyle might even start a whole new fashion wave! *SURFSCOPE* The thrill seeker in you may be toying with the idea of night surfing. If you take the risk, beware of the consequences. Stay away from the reef, make sure the moon above is bright enough for you to see, and no matter what—don't go alone!

VIRGO Aug. 23–Sept. 22 *LOVESCOPE* You love to help out friends but can't understand why no one else wants to return the favor. Stop being the life preserver for everyone. Letting them live their own lives is more help than you may realize. *SURFSCOPE* Don't let opportunities slip away this month—break in slippery new bodyboards by scrubbing them mildly with soap and water before drying and waxing them to help keep you from falling off.

LIBRA Sept. 23–Oct. 22 *LOVESCOPE* Sometimes the things we value most aren't really that valuable when it comes right down to it. Make a list of priorities and re-evaluate them before your goals get drowned by your efforts to do it all! *SURFSCOPE* There's a Libra in "Library." To entertain you between sets, consider bringing a new novel to the beach.

SCORPIO Oct. 23–Nov. 21 *LOVESCOPE* Your possessive streak may be alienating the most important person in your life. Try adding a little length to your ankle leash of love before it snaps altogether. *SURFSCOPE* Always the bargain hunter, Scorpios may be wise to buy a higher-quality used model surfboard instead of a newer less-expensive model.

SAGITTARIUS Nov. 22–Dec. 21 *LOVESCOPE* Your nearest and dearest has been slacking off while you've been the one carrying the entire weight of the relationship on your shoulders. Hold out for a little while longer. The tide will turn in your favor soon enough. *SURFSCOPE* You could get an edge on your fellow surfers by doing more warm-up exercises on the beach before paddling out.

CAPRICORN Dec. 22–Jan. 19 *LOVESCOPE* If you've been out of touch with someone you love dearly, set aside an afternoon for some quiet chat time together. Your relationship will be stronger for it. *SURFSCOPE* Face it—your room is feeling way tired. Why not deck the walls with some cool surfing posters or photos of your favorite pros? The new look will have you stoked!

AQUARIUS Jan. 20–Feb. 18 *LOVESCOPE* Ever heard the old saying, "What doesn't kill us makes us stronger"? You and your significant other are about to face a major challenge, but don't fret. If you're honest about the way you feel, everything will turn out for the best. *SURFSCOPE* When shopping for the right bodyboard, stand it up on its tail and lean it toward you. If it's within an inch of touching your navel, you've found the right size for you!

PISCES Feb. 19–Mar. 20 *LOVESCOPE* If the pace of life is disappointing you, try to remain calm and concentrate on where you're going. Perhaps you'll realize the destination isn't nearly as important as the journey required to get you there. *SURFSCOPE* If you're surfing in unfamiliar territory, find a local to ask about the break. He will likely know the surf and sand like the back of his hand—and you could make a new friend in the process!

ARIES Mar. 21–Apr. 19 *LOVESCOPE* Your tendency to hold back frustration could lead to a major wipeout. An objective third party may be just the sounding board you need to ride your way back to steady shores. *SURFSCOPE* Weather not cooperating? Feeling landlocked? Try joining in some awesome online discussions. The Internet has plenty of surf forums to keep you amped while you're away from the water!

TAURUS Apr. 20–May 20 *LOVESCOPE* There's someone in your realm who thinks so much like you it's downright scary. Just be sure you both don't share the same target for romance—or one of you may suffer a broken heart. *SURFSCOPE* If you're learning a new surfing technique, take your time and don't be intimidated by the pros at the beach. Remember, they were once beginners too.

GEMINI May 21–June 20 *LOVESCOPE* Just when you believe things couldn't get darker, a new sun appears on the love horizon. Once this new dawn breaks, you're sure to be riding high on a tidal wave of romance. *SURFSCOPE* Make sure you're physically ready before participating in an upcoming event. Competition isn't all you have to worry about— Mother Nature could blow you out of the water as well!

CANCER June 21–July 22 *LOVESCOPE* You may feel confused about your feelings for someone, but deep down you already know the answer. Let your conscience guide you and you will be pleased with whatever path you choose to take. *SURFSCOPE* A word of encouragement can do a world of good for a friend who can't stop getting crushed by the cruel waters. Like the motion of the ocean, the smallest bit of kindness you bestow will eventually come right back to you.

Luna Bay

a ♥ ROXY GIRL series

Kanani shoots her a sour look. *She's so impressed with herself,* she thinks.

A thought flashes through Kanani's mind, so fast she can't stop it. It's an image of Rae wiping out, getting pounded, not being able to make it to the surface . . .

Kanani shoves the thought aside. She feels like a dog for even thinking something like that. What has jealousy done to her? She doesn't even know who she is anymore.

With Tuck and David at her side, Kanani watches as Cate, Luna, and Rae paddle out at First Peak. Cate takes off first. It's a beautiful double-overhead wave, fast and furious. She bottom-turns, rips across the face, and pulls out before it collapses with the force of a two-story building.

Kanani, Tuck, and David let out a cheer. It's easy to see why Cate is a three-time world champion. She rips!

Luna takes off next. She pulls off her bottom turn and heads up the face—only to get caught by the lip and flung off her board. Kanani watches, her heart in her throat, until Luna pops out of the soup and is firmly positioned on her surfboard again.

A second later, Rae starts paddling. She catches a powerful grinder and drops in. But her drop becomes a free fall and she can't hold on. The board hits the water and she bounces off like a rag doll. An instant later, the wave collapses on top of her.

Kanani's stomach clenches. Will her fantasy become reality? Will Rae be seriously hurt—or even killed? Kanani holds her breath and counts. One thousand one . . . one thousand two . . .

Cate is paddling toward the white water where Rae disappeared.

One thousand ten . . . one thousand eleven . . .

At one thousand fifteen, Rae's head breaks through the water. She's gasping for breath and she looks pale. But within seconds, she retrieves her board and begins paddling back out.

Kanani lets out a long, shuddering sigh. She doesn't want to watch anymore, not after that image that flashed through her mind. If anything happens to Rae, she'll blame herself. It isn't rational, she knows that. But she can't help it.

"I'm going back to the tent," she says.

"I'll probably join you soon," David says. "My face feels like it's been sandpapered!"

Tuck chuckles. "I'm going to watch a while longer. Then I think I'll check out the other breaks, maybe catch a few waves myself. I'll let you know how it is out there, Kanani."

Kanani nods, grateful that Tuck understands why she isn't surfing First Peak with the other girls. He's a longboarder like her, and competition isn't what motivates him. It's the sun on his shoulders, the wind in his hair, and the waves beneath his board.

When she looks at Tuck, Kanani thinks, *That could be me someday.* Owning a surf shop, running a surf camp, married to a surfer. The only difference is that Kanani doesn't picture herself living in Crescent Cove. If she owns a surf shop someday, it will be in Hawaii. And that husband? Well, she can't help imagining that it's someone like James.

Back at the campsite, Kanani crawls into the tent and zips up the flap. How glorious to be out of the raging wind! She lies back on her sleeping bag and sighs. But almost immediately, James's face pops into her mind. Her heart throbs and she feels that familiar longing.

She remembers the two of them strolling along the sand in the moonlight, looking for sea turtles. Everything was perfect that first night. And when they walked back to camp, he asked, "Got a kiss for the boy who showed you your first Florida sea turtle?"

That night she only gave him a peck on the cheek. If he was here now . . .

"Wake up, girl! The end of the world is coming!"

Kanani's eyes snap open. She jerks up and looks wildly around the tent. Who said that? Or did she dream it?

The flap opens and James pops his head in, laughing like a madman. "I got you good that time!" he whoops.

"James!" Her heart is racing. "What are you doing here?"

"I was surfin' at Monster's Hole."

"Where's that?"

"About a third of a mile offshore on the south side of the inlet. It was crankin'!" He climbs into the tent and grins down at her. "Then I thought, 'What's that pretty Cali Kanani doin'?' So I came by to find out."

When James says her name like that, she ignites like a match. Then all at once she remembers yesterday and the flame is extinguished. "Go away, James," she says, forcing all the emotion out of her voice. "I'm busy."

"Doing what?" he asks. "When I showed up, you looked like you were fast asleep."

"I'm busy, that's all. Please go."

James's face falls. "What's wrong? If I scared you, I'm sorry. I was only foolin', honest."

"It's not that," she begins. "It's just—"

"Wait," he interrupts. "Close your eyes."

Startled, she does as she's told. She feels his finger lightly brush her eyelashes.

"There, you can open your eyes now," he says. "You had some sand in your eyelashes. I didn't want it to get in those pretty eyes."

"Thank you," she says, feeling flustered. How can she give the cold shoulder to someone who's so considerate, so sweet? *But, wait,* she reminds herself. *That's just an act.*

"What do you care about me?" she asks flatly. "I saw you at the mall yesterday. You were holding Rae's hand."

For just a microsecond, James looks like a kid caught with his hand in the cookie jar. Then he leans back on his haunches and nods. "I saw you too, Kanani. You and Francisco."

"Yeah. So?"

"So, you two were hangin' mighty close. Looked like you had some pretty intimate things to say to each other."

"We were talking, that's all," she says. "I was helping him collect money for the Sebastian Inlet Preservation Coalition."

"Well, that's not how it looked to me. You were practically in his lap. I thought you cared about me, Kanani."

Kanani hesitates. Once again, she feels confused, off balance. She didn't do anything wrong, did she? "Of course I care about you," she says. "But you must not care about me. Otherwise, why would you be holding hands with Rae?"

James laughs ruefully. "Seems we've got ourselves a misunderstanding here." He sits down beside her and takes her hand. "Here comes the truth, the whole truth, and nothing but the truth." He takes a deep breath and says, "I was watchin' the movie when the door at the back of the theater opened. I heard a noise, so I turned around. It was Rae. She had tripped and dropped her popcorn and soda. I ran back to help her, and then she sat down beside me.

"We watched the rest of the movie together. There was no flirtin', hand-holding, nothing. We barely said two words to each other. When the film ended, we left the theater."

James's face grows doleful. "That's when I spotted you and Francisco. Your shoulders were touching and you two were laughing like you were sharin' a secret. I guess I got jealous and kinda lost my head. Without thinkin' it through, I just reached down and grabbed Rae's hand, hopin' you would see me. It was wrong—I know that, Kanani—but the truth is I wanted to hurt you just like you hurt me."

Kanani gazes into James's sorrowful eyes. Is he telling the truth? He certainly looks sincere. And, heavens knows, she *wants* to believe him. She hesitates, unsure what to do or say.

James leans closer. He hesitates too, looking as shy and embarrassed as a puppy that just got caught chewing his master's favorite shoe.

Kanani can't help but smile. And that's when he kisses her—a soft, soulful kiss that sends her reeling.

"Kanani," he whispers, "please forgive me. What I did, I did because of how I feel for you."

She nods, too overwhelmed to speak.

He grins and hugs her tight. Then he pulls back and says, "You need to get out of this musty old tent. Whaddaya say we go jet-skiing?"

"Jet-skiing?" she gasps. "In this weather?"

"You know it, girl! I've jet-skied in hurricane surf way bigger than this. It's a rush!"

"But . . . isn't it dangerous?"

"Not with me at the controls." He pauses, studying her worried face. "Look, we'll take a two-person WaveRunner. I'll be doin' the drivin'. All you have to do is hang on."

"Well . . ."

"I want to do something nice to make up for hurtin' you yesterday. Come on, I know we're goin' to have fun out there. Say yes, Cali Kanani. Please?"

How can she refuse? In just a couple of days, she'll be returning to California. She may never see James again. She can't pass up a chance to be with him now.

Her heart is revving like a two-stroke engine as she whispers, "Okay, James. Let's go."

11

Kanani and James run up the dock, hand in hand. Kanani's heart is pounding—partly because she's about to go jet-skiing in a tropical storm, partly just because James is holding her hand.

James opens the door of the Sebastian Inlet Water Sports rentals shop and they walk inside. But there's nobody behind the counter. They go back out and look around. Nobody on the dock either.

While James walks up the dock, calling Francisco's name, Kanani checks out the WaveRunners. They're bigger than jet skis, more like miniboats. They have a seat like a motorcycle, just big enough for two people.

James returns. "Not many people renting jet skis today," he remarks with a chuckle. "Francisco probably stepped out for a while."

"So we can't go out," Kanani says, half disappointed and half relieved.

"Sure we can. Francisco won't mind if I borrow one of these." He walks to the edge of the dock and climbs on one of the WaveRunners.

"Wait," Kanani says. "Are you sure it's all right? I mean, shouldn't we at least leave a note?"

James shrugs. "I've borrowed his uncle's boats before. It's no biggie. Besides, we won't be out long." He starts the engine and unties the line. "Hop on, Pretty One."

Kanani hesitates. She doesn't have a good feeling about this. But James is holding out his hand, smiling that sweet, dimpled smile. Pushing her doubts aside, she climbs on the WaveRunner and puts her arms around his waist.

"Hmm, I like the feel of that," he says, leaning back and resting his head on her shoulder.

She can smell his minty shampoo and feel his warm breath on her cheek. Her heart does a 360. Still resting against her, he steers away from the dock and heads toward the Indian River.

The wind in the Inlet is intense, whipping Kanani's thick mane of hair like a flag. But it's only a gentle zephyr compared to the raging wind that's whistling across the open lagoon. Kanani gapes in disbelief at the rolling whitecaps.

There are only a couple of other boats in sight, both

of them much bigger than the WaveRunner. But before Kanani can ask James if he's sure he knows what he's doing, he shouts, "Woo-ee!" and opens the throttle.

They roar across the lagoon, smacking into the chop. The WaveRunner bucks like an angry bronco. Kanani gasps and grabs James's waist in a death grip.

"Let's see what this baby can do!" he yells.

He skids into a high-speed turn, then guns the engine. The WaveRunner rockets forward. They hit a rolling whitecap and fly into the air.

Kanani holds her breath. They seem to be airborne forever. Then . . . *smack!* The WaveRunner slams down hard. Kanani's chin whacks against James's shoulder. But there's no time to nurse her wounds. Another wave looms ahead, bigger than the last.

"Yeah, baby!" James screams as they lift off.

Kanani closes her eyes and presses her head against James's shoulder. She's never been so scared in her life—or so exhilarated! She's on a galloping horse, blindfolded, and someone else is holding the reins. It's insane, but there's no turning back now.

"Yes!" she shrieks as they lift off.

Suddenly, a gust of wind slams the WaveRunner, causing it to list wildly to the left. James leans hard to the right, and Kanani follows his lead. He revs the accelerator as they land and they take off with a jerk, barely managing to hang on.

And then, all at once the skies open and it starts to pour. James slows down. Kanani pushes her hair out of her eyes and looks around. The rain is so intense she can barely see five feet in front of her.

"Let's go back," she shouts in his ear.

"I've got a better idea," he replies.

He turns east and cruises across the lagoon. He's not gunning it anymore, not even trying to catch air. Kanani blinks and wipes the rain off her face.

"Where are we going?"

"You'll see."

A few minutes later, Kanani spies something dark and low on the horizon. The water is less choppy here; the wind less fierce. As they move closer, she sees they're heading toward a line of mangrove trees.

"James—" she begins.

He turns his head and puts a finger to his lips. Then he steers the WaveRunner into a narrow channel between two rows of mangrove trees.

"James, you're not supposed to drive powerboats in here," she says anxiously. "There are rare birds living in the mangroves, and manatees."

"Don't worry. We'll take it slow, I promise."

"But James—"

"Hush," he says, cutting her off. "I want to show you something."

The channel twists and turns. Mangroves grow on

either side, their roots sticking out of the water like the knobby brown knees of a thousand swamp sprites. The rain is softer now, a gentle patter. The shriek of an unseen bird splits the air.

Kanani stares with wonder at the mangrove forest. It's magical, like something out of a fantasy novel. She knows they're not supposed to be riding here, but she can't bring herself to ask James to turn back. It's just too special.

James brings the WaveRunner to a stop. "Here," he says, pointing down at the water. "This is the spot where I found it."

"Found what?" Kanani asks.

"This." He reaches into the pocket of his bathing suit and pulls out an ancient-looking gold coin. "It's a Spanish piece of eight," he says in a hushed voice. "Almost three hundred years old."

"You found that *here?*" she exclaims.

He nods. "Way back in 1715, eleven Spanish galleons sank in a hurricane near here. You know what was in those ships, Kanani? Gold coins and ingots plundered from the Incas of South America."

James turns the battered coin over in his hand. "The survivors set up camps and tried to salvage the wrecks," he continues. "But they didn't get everything, not by a long shot. A lot of that gold is still out here in the water, waiting to be found."

He pauses. "One day I was kayaking back here and I saw something gleaming in the water. I dove down to see what it was." He grins. "When I came back up, I had myself a little piece of history."

He reaches for Kanani's hand and lays the coin carefully in her palm. "It's beautiful, isn't it?" he says.

She nods, too awed to speak.

"I want you to have it."

"Me?" she gasps.

"To remember me by."

"But James—"

He leans his head against her shoulder, silencing her. "You're goin' home in a couple days, back to your regular life. Pretty soon your trip to Florida will be nothin' but a distant memory. But I hope once in a while, you'll look at this coin and think about me."

"Oh, James," she breathes, "I will."

"That's good because I'll be thinkin' about you, Cali Kanani. Every single day."

Kanani wraps her arms around James and hugs him tight. Her heart aches like an open wound. Oh, how can she ever leave him?

12

Kanani is clutching the gold coin tightly in her hand as James drives the WaveRunner back to the dock. They're climbing off when the door of the rental shop flies open and a middle-aged man runs out.

"So it was you!" he shouts. "I should have known it. Only you would be *loco* enough to go out in this weather."

"Hi, Luis," James says with a grin. "I want you to meet my friend Kanani. Kanani, this is Francisco's uncle. He owns the—"

"And who gave you permission to borrow one of my WaveRunners?" Luis demands, ignoring Kanani. "You don't do that without checking with me first."

"Francisco said it would be okay," James declares innocently. "I'm sorry if I did anything wro—"

"Francisco? Wait until I get my hands on that boy! I'll tan his hide from now until Sunday!"

"But James—" Kanani begins.

"Gotta go, Luis," James says, cutting her off. "Kanani's got a pressing engagement."

He grabs her hand and starts running up the dock. She stumbles after him, wondering what's going on. When they get out of sight of Luis, James starts to laugh. "That was a close one!"

"What's going on?" Kanani asks. "I thought you said you'd borrowed jet skis from Francisco's uncle lots of times."

"Well, I might have exaggerated just a tad," he says, cracking up.

Kanani frowns. "Is Francisco going to get in trouble?"

"Oh, lighten up, Kanani," James scolds. "It's no big deal. Just a joke, really."

"But—"

He silences her with a kiss. "I'll see you soon, okay?" he whispers in her ear.

"When?" she asks, trying to get control of her buckling knees.

"Soon. I promise." He steps back and gazes at her seriously. "You got the coin?" She opens her hand to show him. "Good." He grins. Then he jogs off toward the jetties.

. . .

Kanani walks back to camp, daydreaming about James—the feel of her arms around his waist, his head on her shoulder, his kiss. She's so distracted, she's almost at the campsite before she realizes the tents are gone.

She stops, perplexed, then walks closer. Luna, David, and Rae are helping Tuck and Cate load their belongings into the SUV.

"What's going on?" she calls, running up to join them. "Are we leaving?"

"Where have you been?" Tuck asks. "We've been looking all over for you."

Kanani considers telling the truth, but somehow she has a feeling Tuck and Cate wouldn't like the idea of her jet-skiing during a tropical storm. "I . . . I was with James," she says at last.

Kanani sees Rae's head spin around, notices the shocked look on her face. She knows she shouldn't feel pleased, but she can't help it.

"The tropical storm has been upgraded to a hurricane," Cate says. "We have to move inland right away."

Tuck is strapping the surfboards to the roof. "The park is closing. Fortunately, I found us a room in a motel out by I-95."

Kanani feels a little numb. She can't believe she and

James were jet-skiing in near-hurricane weather. They could have been killed!

"Okay, everybody, get in," Cate announces. "We're outta here."

Tuck drives out of the park and they head up A1A to I-95. Wind rattles the SUV, and rain pounds the windows so hard the wipers are worthless. The roads are covered with water, making driving slow and tedious. Every few minutes, another police car or ambulance roars by, lights flashing and sirens wailing.

"I can't believe this is happening," Luna says glumly. "A few days ago it was hot and sunny."

"And we were training for a surf contest," Rae adds.

"This is nothing," David says. "The National Hurricane Center is only predicting a Category One hurricane. That means winds between seventy-five and ninety-five miles per hour. You want to see a real hurricane, try Category Five. That's winds over a hundred and fifty-five miles per hour!"

"Stop it," Luna grumbles. "You sound like a weather report."

"I'm just trying to keep everyone informed. We can expect coastal flooding and minor building and pier damage, but that's about it."

"What about the surf?" Rae asks.

"Is that all you can think about?" Kanani mutters.

Rae shoots her a withering look.

"It'll be huge by tonight," David replies. "Probably fifteen feet or bigger."

Rae looks stressed. "Are you serious?"

"Who wants to join me on dawn patrol?" Luna jokes. "We'll catch a few tubes before breakfast."

But Rae isn't laughing. She looks out the window and bites her nails.

"How do you know so much about hurricanes, David?" Kanani asks.

"I live in Florida, remember? It's a fact of life around here."

"You think this is serious?" Luna asks. "We have earthquakes in California. Now *that's* serious."

"They're both serious, okay?" Rae snaps.

"Will you kids stop snipping at each other," Cate says. "I know you're disappointed, but let's not take it out on each other."

After that, a stony silence falls on the car. Tuck turns on the radio and they listen to the announcer talk about floods, wind damage, road closings, and evacuation warnings until they get to the motel.

"We're all going to stay in here?" Luna gasps as her father unlocks the door to the room. "You've got to be kidding!"

Kanani walks in and looks around. There are two double beds, that's it.

"This was the only room I could find," Tuck explains. "Everything's booked."

"We have our sleeping bags," Cate points out. "It won't be a problem."

"Who gets the beds?" Rae asks.

"We'll draw straws for them," Tuck says. "Now stop complaining and help me unload the bags."

Soon the room is crowded with suitcases and people.

"You can take turns calling your parents," Cate says. "Here, use my calling card."

Kanani is the first to use the phone. When her mother answers, Kanani's heart soars. It surprises her and she has to smile. She didn't know how much she missed her parents until she heard their voices. Even annoying Cameron sounds pretty good. Fortunately, her family hasn't been watching the news and they don't know about the hurricane. She breaks it to them gently, down-playing the danger.

"We miss you, sweetheart," Mom says. "The house feels empty without you."

"I miss you too," Kanani says, and she means it. Maybe her parents aren't hot Hawaiian surfers—or athletes of any kind—but she loves them and she knows they love her too. And that feels pretty good.

When everyone has made their phone calls, David grabs the remote and turns on Cartoon Network. Luna and Kanani play Boggle, Tuck reads a longboard-ing magazine, and Cate goes into the bathroom to take a shower.

Kanani glances at Rae. She's standing at the window,

staring out at the parking lot with a worried look on her face. "Can we watch the Weather Channel?" Rae asks after a minute.

"I'm sick of thinking about the weather," Luna says.

"Relax, Rae," David adds. "We're out of the flood zone. Nothing's going to happen to us."

Ignoring them, Rae snatches the remote control off the bed and switches quickly through the channels.

"Hey!" David and Luna cry in unison.

The Weather Channel clicks on. They're showing huge storm surf battering a pier. "Hurricane Ana is bringing high surf and extensive damage to the coastal areas of eastern Florida," the announcer is saying. "Stay inside and, most importantly, do not go near the ocean."

Luna leans over and uses the controls on the TV to switch the channel. "I'm sick of hurricanes," she exclaims. "I want mindless entertainment!"

David laughs, but Rae scowls and throws down the remote. Then she turns to Kanani. "I need to talk to you—outside."

Kanani hesitates. Rae wants to talk to *her?* This can't be good. Rae heads for the door and Kanani, not knowing what else to do, reluctantly follows her. They step outside and stand under the overhang, watching the rain pour down.

"Did J.T. tell you what he's planning to do this afternoon?" Rae asks.

"No," Kanani answers. "Why?"

"Well, he told *me*."

Rae saw James today? Kanani is confused. "When was this?"

"This morning. He came in from surfing Monster's Hole and stopped by First Peak to look for me."

Kanani's heart sinks. She thought James had come directly to the campsite looking for her. But he had been with Rae first. "Oh," is all she can manage to mutter.

"He said he's going surfing," Rae announces.

"Surfing?" Instantly, Kanani's jealousy is replaced by another emotion—fear. "No way. In a hurricane?"

"He had no way of knowing the storm would be upgraded to a hurricane. And Kanani, he's out there somewhere. Who knows what's happened to him. I mean, J.T. is a good surfer, but he's not *that* good."

"I know. And the surf is macking."

Rae nods. "Did you hear what David said? They're expecting fifteen-foot waves, maybe bigger."

"Maybe he didn't go out," Kanani says. "Maybe he heard the weather report and changed his mind." But even as she says it, she knows it isn't true. James didn't have any hesitation about jet-skiing in a tropical storm. In fact, he told her he'd jet-skied in hurricane surf.

Rae is thinking the same thing. "J.T.'s a daredevil," she says. "If he heard the storm was upgraded to a hurricane it would just make him more eager to go out."

Kanani bites her lower lip. "We have to stop him," she declares.

"That's what I've been telling myself," Rae agrees. "But how? We don't know where he is."

"Maybe we can find him."

"How?"

"Through Francisco. James might have told him where he was headed. I mean, it's a long shot, but . . ."

"Look, there's a phone booth," Rae says, pointing through the rain. "Let's call the rental place and see if Francisco is there."

They make a mad dash to the phone booth and call information. But when they punch in the number of the rental place, all they get is a recording. "You've reached Sebastian Inlet Water Sports," Francisco's voice says. "We're open from seven A.M. until six P.M. Tuesday through Sunday . . ."

"What now?" Kanani asks.

Rae bites her fingernail, considering. "I say we go back to Sebastian Inlet and look around. We might find James, or Francisco, or at least someone who knows where they are."

"You think Tuck and Cate will let us do that?" Kanani asks anxiously.

"No," Rae says. "But I think we should do it anyway. We have to, if we really care about J.T."

"James," Kanani corrects.

Rae purses her lips and starts to say something, then stops herself and shrugs. "Whatever. Are you with me, Kanani?" She holds out her pinky expectantly.

Kanani thinks it over. Rae's plan is crazy, and possibly dangerous. But when Kanani pictures James paddling out in fifteen-foot killer hurricane surf, she feels sick inside. What if something happens to him? She'll never forgive herself.

She bites the inside of her cheek. A few minutes ago, she would have insisted she never wanted to do anything with Rae again. But now . . .

"Okay," she says, slipping her pinky around Rae's and squeezing tight. "Let's do it."

13

"We're going for a walk, okay?" Rae asks Cate.

"A walk? In this storm?"

Kanani crosses her fingers behind her back. "I saw a Starbucks down the road. We thought since this place is so boring we'd hang out there for a while."

Cate considers. "I don't know. It's crazy out there. The wind, the rain, the traffic . . ."

"Please," Rae pleads. "We're going stir-crazy in here. We'll be careful, honest."

Cate sighs. "Okay, okay. But don't stay gone too long. And when you come back, bring me a latte. Tuck, you want something from Starbucks?"

"For sure," he says, glancing up from his magazine. "Make mine a mocha."

"Be sure to ask Luna and David," Cate says.

But Kanani doesn't want to ask them. What if they decide they want to come along? But Rae walks over and talks to them, then returns with Luna's raincoat for Kanani to wear.

"Oh, wow, thanks," Kanani says. They walk outside and close the door. "I'm glad Luna and David didn't want to join us."

Rae grins. "I told them you couldn't find your wallet and we were going out to the car to look for it."

"Liar," Kanani says.

"What about you?" She mimics Kanani's voice. " 'There's a Starbucks down the road.' "

"All right, all right. So what now? Do you think there's a bus to Sebastian Inlet?"

"How should I know? Let's ask at the motel office."

In the office, a wrinkled, henna-haired woman with a cigarette dangling from her mouth looks up from behind the desk.

"Can we get a bus from here to Sebastian Inlet?" Rae asks.

The woman barks a laugh. "No bus service in this weather, dearie. Besides, you don't want to go near the coast. Hurricane's coming, you know."

"Right," Kanani says. "It's just . . . we're looking for someone."

The woman shakes her head, knocking ashes from her cigarette onto the desk. "Only possibility is a taxi, if you can find one that'll take you." She hands the girls a phone book and a portable phone. "Good luck."

Kanani consults the phone book and Rae makes the calls. After five failed tries, they find a taxi company that's willing to drive them to the inlet.

Returning the phone, they hurry outside to wait. Ten minutes later, they're still waiting. Kanani glances uncomfortably at Rae.

What am I doing? she asks herself. *Rae stole my boyfriend—or tried to anyway. Now we're joining forces to find him. Am I nuts or what?*

Rae looks just as uneasy. "I should have made J.T. promise me he wouldn't surf," she mutters, half to herself.

"I doubt he would have listened," Kanani remarks.

"How do you know?"

"I know him, believe me."

Rae doesn't look impressed. "If you know him so well, why did he come looking for me this morning instead of you?"

Kanani opens her mouth to answer but just then the taxi pulls up. "Sebastian Inlet," she tells the driver as they climb in.

"Don't know if I can get there," he replies. "There's a

lot of flooding near the coast. Besides, isn't the state park closed?"

"Just drive us as close as you can," Rae says.

The taxi pulls away from the motel, moving slowly through the wet streets. Kanani rides in silence. In her mind, she's picturing James paddling out in monster hurricane surf. The thought leaves her limp with fear. She glances at Rae, who sits frowning down at her hands. Is she thinking the same thing?

The taxi drives onto the A1A. The wind is whipping the ocean into a gray froth. A wave crashes against the pilings, splashing spray across the road.

A road sign for Sebastian Inlet reminds Kanani that they'll soon have to pay the taxi driver. "Rae," she whispers, "I didn't think about money. How much do you have?"

Rae looks stricken. She pulls out her wallet. "Ten dollars and change. How about you?"

Kanani is riffling through her backpack. "Twenty-two and some pennies." She leans forward to check the meter. Twenty-nine dollars. She lets out a sigh. "We're cool," she tells Rae. "But you owe me."

"Okay, okay. Remind me later."

The driver stops at the entrance to the state park. A ranger steps out of the kiosk. "We're closed," she says. "No one's allowed in."

"We . . . uh, we work with Francisco," Rae blurts

out. "At . . . at the water sports rental place on the dock, you know? He told us to meet him here."

"He and his uncle are loading up their boats and heading out," the ranger replies. "They didn't say anything about anyone coming to help them."

"They didn't?" Rae exclaims. She looks sincerely amazed. "But Francisco called us."

"Ask Luis," Kanani says boldly, praying the ranger won't actually do it. "He'll confirm what we're saying."

Luis seems to be the magic word. "I'll drive you over," the ranger says.

Kanani and Rae pay the taxi driver and follow the ranger to her truck. Kanani's heart is skittering like a rabbit with a coyote on its tail. What if Luis remembers her from this morning and tells the ranger to arrest her for taking his WaveRunner without permission?

But it's Francisco who sees them first. He's standing on the back of a truck, strapping a row of kayaks to an overhead rack.

"Kanani! Rae! What are you doing here?" he asks in disbelief.

The girls jump out of the ranger's car. "Didn't think we'd make it, did you?" Kanani says, faking a laugh. "But we're here, just like you asked us to be."

"Huh?" he says blankly. Then a look of understanding crosses his face. "Oh! Yes. Terrific!" He turns to the ranger. "Thanks, Judy. Everything is A-OK."

She looks skeptical, but says nothing. "Okay, Francisco. Just get out of here as soon as you can, all right?"

Francisco nods and tips his Florida Marlins cap as Ranger Judy drives away. Then he turns to Kanani and Rae. "*Qué pasa?*" he demands. "What in the world are you doing here?"

"Do you know where J.T. is?" Rae asks.

"T-Bone? No. Why?"

"He told me he was going surfing this afternoon," Rae says.

"That sounds like him," Francisco says, shaking his head. "That fool will do anything for a thrill."

Kanani fears Francisco is right, but she doesn't want to hear anything bad about James right now. "We have to stop him," she says. "Do you know where he is?"

Francisco shakes his head. "Not a clue. But I'd like to find him. I've got a few words to say to him about what happened this morning."

He looks at Kanani significantly. She winces, remembering how James lied to Luis, telling him that Francisco gave them permission to borrow the WaveRunner.

Rae looks at them quizzically. Kanani knows she's wondering what Francisco is talking about. But there's no time to get into all that now.

"Do you have his phone number?" Kanani asks. "Maybe his parents know where he is."

Francisco sighs. "Come on inside. I'll call his house."

On the way into the shop, they pass Francisco's uncle. He stops and stares at the girls. "What the—" he begins. "Who—" Then his eyes rest on Kanani. *"You!"*

"It's okay, *tio*," Francisco says. "I'll explain everything later. Just finish tying down the kayaks, okay? I'll be out in a second."

Luis scowls but continues on his way. Francisco dials the phone, waits, then shakes his head. "Just the answering machine. His parents probably drove inland. T-Bone might be with them."

"But if he isn't . . ." Rae's voice trails off.

"Francisco," Kanani pleads, "I'm worried. What should we do?"

He pauses, thinking it over. "James can probably take care of himself. But if it will make you feel better, we can drive down the coast and try to find him."

"Oh, Francisco, would you really?" Kanani cries.

"Sure. But I can't leave until my uncle and I load the truck," he warns.

"We'll help you," Rae offers.

Kanani nods, eager to begin searching for James. "Let's do it," she says.

Kanani rolls down the window of Francisco's VW van and peers out at First Peak. The waves are humping monsters, as tall as houses. "Looks like there are a few people out there," she says, squinting through the rain, "but I can barely make them out."

A dark figure comes running toward them through the rain. As he approaches, they can see he's carrying a surfboard. "J.T.?" Rae calls out.

But no, it's a brawny guy in his twenties. "Who?" he asks.

"Do you know James Tibbets?" Kanani asks.

"Yeah, I know him. But I haven't seen him. Try Wabasso."

"What's Wabasso?" Kanani asks Francisco as the man runs off.

"Another surf spot. It's about ten miles south of here."

"Let's go," Rae says, putting up her window.

Francisco drives slowly across the flooded parking lot. Kanani shakes out her tired arms. She spent the last half hour helping to push jet skis and WaveRunners into Uncle Luis's truck and she's worn out. Luckily, Luis was too worried about his boats to yell at Kanani. All he managed was a few muttered words about "that Tibbits boy and his girlfriends."

Francisco drives south on A1A. The swells are hitting the pilings regularly now, spraying buckets of water onto the road. Francisco leans forward, staring intently out the front window. Suddenly, something that looks like a log flies past the van.

Kanani shrieks and plasters herself against the seat. "What was that?" she cries.

"Who knows?" Francisco answers grimly. "Driftwood, a piece of a boat, a sign maybe. The wind just grabs stuff and sends it flying."

They get off A1A at Wabasso and drive to the beach. Once again, there are a few surfers braving the treacherous waters. But whether one of them is James—well, who can tell? Francisco and the girls ask some locals who are standing under a shelter watching the action. Two of them know James by sight, but they haven't seen him all day.

"This is crazy," Francisco says. "We're not going to find him. And even if we did, how would we get his attention to call him in?"

"But we can't give up!" Rae insists.

"Yes we can. As long as you're in my van, I'm responsible for you. And I'm not going to risk your lives driving up and down the coast in the middle of a hurricane."

"But—" Kanani begins.

"No buts," Francisco says firmly. "We could get caught in a flood, or blown off the road, or even hit by flying debris. Besides, another hour and the highway's going to be underwater. What will we do then?"

Neither Kanani nor Rae has an answer for that. So Francisco drives back toward the highway. But Kanani can't stop thinking about James. Where is he? With his parents in some safe, dry place? Or out in the ocean, risking his life in hurricane surf?

Kanani starts to realize that a lot of time has passed since they left the motel. Cate and Tuck must be getting worried. A look of panic washes over her face, but she tries to keep her focus on James instead. After all, this *is* a life-or-death situation. Hopefully, Luna's parents will be understanding. What's important right now is making sure James is safe and sound.

"What's that up ahead?" Rae asks, breaking into Kanani's thoughts.

Kanani leans forward, peering at the flashing red lights in the distance. "Looks like police cars," she says anxiously.

As they drive closer, they see a barricade blocking the entrance to the A1A. "Uh-oh," Francisco mutters.

"What's going on?" Kanani asks.

Before he can answer, a cop pulls them over. "Hello, folks. The highway is closed due to high surf."

"I guess we'll have to take I-95," Francisco says.

"I doubt you can get there," the cop answers. "There's been a lot of flooding throughout the Wabasso area."

"Thank you, Officer." Francisco puts up his window and backs up. He drives east toward I-95, but within minutes they hit another roadblock.

"What now?" Kanani asks.

"I think we're spending the night in Wabasso," he says.

"Are you serious?" Rae asks incredulously. "We can't get back to the motel?"

"Not unless you've got a boat." He shrugs. "I've got a friend who'll let us stay over. He lives on the beach."

"The beach?" Kanani gasps. "That's the last place we want to be now."

"His house is all concrete, built on tall pilings. I rode out the last hurricane there. It was pretty cool, actually."

"But—" Kanani begins.

"It's either that or the Red Cross shelter," Francisco says. "Take your pick."

Kanani and Rae glance at each other. "The beach," they say in unison.

14

"Is that it?" Kanani asks, peering out the rain-soaked window at a beach house built on concrete pilings.

"Yep," Francisco replies. "We made it."

Kanani lets out a sigh of relief. They've spent the last forty minutes crawling at a snail's pace through driving rain, pounding winds, and flooded streets. Once Francisco lost sight of the road and veered into a muddy ditch. It took all three of them to push the van out.

"I can't believe it's nearly seven o'clock," Rae declares.

"It feels like we left the motel a week ago!" Kanani says. She's wet, mud-spattered, and exhausted. Plus, she can't remember the last time she ate anything. Was it those potato chips they munched in the SUV when Tuck and Cate drove to the motel? The memory makes her stomach grumble.

"Now let's just hope someone's home," Francisco says, climbing out of the van.

Kanani and Rae follow and together they run up the stairs to the beach house. James knocks on the front door. After what seems like forever, it opens. Pounding rock music fills the air. A boy with shoulder-length brown hair appears and breaks into a grin.

"Sisco, how are you, man? Come on in!"

Gratefully, they wipe their feet and step inside. Whoa! It's like stepping into another world. The room is filled with people, talking, laughing, eating, dancing. There are teenagers, little kids, adults, even an elderly couple. The only light comes from the flashlights the partygoers are holding. Now the rock song ends and a throbbing salsa number begins. The crowd lets out a whoop and everyone begins to dance and sing along.

"Rob, these are my friends Kanani and Rae," Francisco says. "Girls, this is my buddy Rob. He lives here."

"Welcome to our hurricane party!" Rob shouts over the music. "Make yourself at home."

"Thanks!" Rae shouts back.

"Can we use your phone?" Kanani asks. She glances at Rae. "We have to call Tuck and Cate and tell them where we are."

Rae grimaces. "This isn't going to be pretty."

"The phone lines are down," Rob says. "But you can

use my cell." He hands the phone to Kanani. "Better go to the back of the house where it's quieter."

Kanani and Rae make their way through the crowded living room. The kitchen is filled with people too, but down the hallway they find an empty bedroom. They step inside and close the door. The only light comes from a candle on the bedside table.

"You want to call?" Kanani asks, offering the phone to Rae.

"You're better at that kind of thing," she says with a pleading look.

"All right, all right." She takes a deep breath and dials.

"Hello?" It's Cate's voice.

"Hi, Cate. It's me, Kanani."

"Where in the world are you?" Cate practically screams. "Where's Rae? Are you all right?"

"She's right here. We're fine, honest." Kanani explains everything that's happened over the last several hours—everything except the hurricane party, that is. Somehow she has a feeling Cate wouldn't quite understand the concept of partying through a hurricane. She's not sure she understands it herself. "We're staying in Wabasso, at Francisco's friend's house," she explains. "Francisco will drive us back as soon as the roads are open."

There's a moment of suspenseful silence. When Cate

finally speaks, it's in a quiet voice that's much scarier than her screaming one. "You girls are in so much trouble. Big trouble. What do you think your parents are going to say when they find out you lied to Tuck and me, and then ran off in the middle of a hurricane?"

Kanani doesn't want to think about that. "Do you have to tell them?" she asks in a small voice.

"I'm not going to even bother to answer that," Cate snaps. "Now stay put and call me in the morning. Oh, and give me your number there."

Kanani gives her Rob's cell phone number and hangs up. "We might as well throw ourselves into the hurricane," she tells Rae. "Cate's going to kill us anyway."

Rae manages a weak laugh. Then she sighs and sits down on the bed. "I don't feel like going out there," she says, tipping her head in the direction of the living room. "I'm not exactly in a party mood."

"Me either," Kanani agrees, taking a seat on the rug. "I can't stop thinking about James. I just wish we could be sure he's all right."

"I guess the Coast Guard is patrolling the beaches," Rae says, but her voice doesn't sound too confident. "They'll rescue anyone who needs help, right?"

"I guess so. If they get there in time."

"Oh, Kanani," Rae confides, "I'm scared. J.T. wasn't taking the storm seriously, I could tell."

"I know what you mean," Kanani answers. "He

doesn't think about how dangerous things are. He took me jet-skiing on the lagoon this morning and he was acting like it was just another day at the beach."

"You went jet-skiing with J.T. this morning?" Rae gasps.

Kanani can't help feeling a tiny bit pleased. *You're not the only one who spent time with James this morning,* she thinks smugly. But all she says is, "We took out one of the WaveRunners. It was so windy, we were practically blown into the water."

"I—I don't understand why he asked you to go with him," Rae says, her voice trembling. "Why didn't he ask me?"

As she gazes into Rae's troubled face, Kanani's pleasure is replaced by pity. "Rae," she says gently, "I know this is hard to hear, but James is in love with me. He told me so."

"What do you mean? What did he say?"

"Well, he didn't use the word *love* exactly," Kanani admits. "But he told me he was going to miss me when I went home to California. He said he'd be thinking about me every single day."

"He told me that too," Rae retorts.

"Impossible!" Kanani says. "Anyway, he didn't mean it the way he meant it with me."

"Oh, yeah?" Rae snaps. She doesn't look hurt anymore. Just mad. "How do you know?"

"Because he hugged me. He kissed me too. Not just once—a bunch of times."

"You're not the only one who's been kissed by J.T. The first time was the morning we went kayaking. And that day we went jet-skiing and he took you back to the dock—he kissed me then too."

Is Rae making this up? Kanani wonders. If she isn't . . . well, Kanani doesn't want to think about that. It just hurts too much.

Finally, she decides she has to make Rae understand, once and for all, that James is hers. She reaches into the zippered pocket of her backpack and takes out the gold coin. "James gave me something to prove his love," she says. "Something really special. Look." She opens her fist, revealing the Spanish piece of eight.

Rae's jaw drops. "Where did you get that?"

"I told you. From James."

Frantically, Rae stuffs her hand in the pocket of her shorts and pulls something out. Kanani's throat tightens. It's another gold coin!

Rae hands her the coin. It looks exactly like hers! "James gave you this?" she says, her voice cracking.

Rae nods. "This morning."

Just then, the door opens and Francisco looks in. "Did you get through to your friend's mom and dad?"

Kanani nods, but she can't stop staring at the two matching coins.

Francisco notices them and smiles. "I see you've been to the Crow's Nest."

"What?"

"The souvenir shop in Melbourne Beach. They sell reproductions of old Spanish coins there."

Rae stares at him. "You mean these aren't real gold?"

Francisco laughs. "Who told you that?"

Kanani winces. "James," she admits.

"That guy is such a practical joker!" Francisco exclaims, shaking his head. "Those coins cost about two bucks apiece, tops."

Kanani feels tears welling up in her eyes. How could James have lied to her like that? She just can't understand it.

But the gold coin isn't the only thing he lied about, she realizes with dismay. He lied when he said she was pretty, when he said he cared about her, and when he told her he'd think about her every day after she returned to California. In fact, she wouldn't be surprised if every single thing he'd ever said to her was a lie.

"Are you two ready to come out and join the party?" Francisco asks.

Kanani looks up. Can he see the tears in her eyes? Embarrassed, she forces a laugh and says, "Sure, we'll be there. We just need a couple of minutes alone."

"Okay," he answers, smiling. "I'll be waiting for you."

Francisco closes the door and Kanani turns to Rae.

"James isn't in love with either of us," she says, wiping her eyes.

Rae nods sadly. "He was just stringing us along, messing with our minds. He's probably got five or six other girls he's treating the same way."

"What an actor! I mean, he seemed so sincere, so real."

"I know. But that's not what bothers me the most," Rae says. "It's the way James turned us against each other. I mean, when you told me he took you out on the WaveRunner, I was so jealous I could hardly breathe. For a minute there, I was starting to think I hated you."

"Rae, I have a confession to make," Kanani says slowly. "When I was watching you surf yesterday, I was hoping you'd wipe out, wishing for it, even. There was a moment when I imagined you going under and never coming up, because then I would have James all to myself." She looks at her friend pleadingly. "That's so sick. Can you ever forgive me?"

Rae smiles. "If you can forgive me."

Kanani stands up and opens her arms. Rae jumps off the bed and the two girls hug. Tears well up in Kanani's eyes, but this time her heart is filled with joy, not sadness.

"Our friendship is so much more important than some stupid boy," she says.

Rae rolls her eyes. "Especially when the boy is James J.T. T-Bone Tibbets."

"We should have known better than to trust a guy with so many aliases!"

Rae cracks up. "They'll come in handy when he starts his life of crime."

"Didn't I tell you?" Kanani says. "He already started. This morning he took the WaveRunner without Francisco's permission. When Luis found out, James told him Francisco had said it was all right."

Rae shakes her head. "What a loser. If only he wasn't so hot."

"Tell me about it. Those dimples are to die for."

They fall silent, thinking about adorable, infuriating James. Gradually, Kanani becomes aware of the thumping R & B music that's wafting in from the living room. She looks at Rae and smiles. "I think I'm finally getting into a party mood."

"You want to check it out?"

Kanani shrugs. "Why not?"

Rae holds out her pinky and Kanani squeezes it tightly with her own. "Let's go, girlfriend," she says with a grin.

15

Kanani's eyes pop open. Where is she? What time is it? She sits bolt upright and looks around her. Then she sees Rae sleeping peacefully beside her on the bed and suddenly everything comes back to her. They're at the house of Francisco's friend, Rob. Last night was the hurricane party.

Kanani rests her head against the pillow and smiles. The party was a total blast! They were up half the night, talking, laughing, and dancing. The music was an eclectic mix of rock, R & B, rap, and salsa. The food was eclectic too—everything from chips and dips to Cuban-style garlic chicken to sushi.

Kanani chuckles, remembering how Francisco tried to teach her salsa dancing. It was so different from the dancing she was used to. Instead of doing her own thing, she had to follow Francisco and match his steps. She wasn't very good at it, but he didn't seem to mind. And when he held her in his arms and they swayed their bodies to the sizzling beat—well, she didn't mind either!

Kanani stretches beneath the blanket. It's weird to realize that while they were partying, a hurricane was raging outside. The windows were shuttered, but Francisco showed her how she could peek through the gaps and see what was happening on the beach. The waves were slamming against the sand, sending churning water all the way up to the pilings. And the wind—it was mind-boggling how hard it was blowing! Every once in a while, something big—a piece of wood, a lawn chair, a garbage can—would fly right past the window. Once they actually saw a bicycle whiz by!

But that was last night. Now it's strangely still and Kanani realizes the roaring wind has stopped. Jumping out of bed, she opens the curtains and peers through the shutters. It's not raining anymore. The sky is still gray, but she can see a patch of blue on the horizon. The hurricane is over!

"Wake up, Rae," Kanani says, shaking her friend. "It's morning."

Rae's eyes flutter open. Slowly, her mouth curls into a smile. "Good party."

"Totally. Who was that guy you were dancing with?"

"His name is Cody. He goes to school with Rob." She sits up and rubs her eyes. "You and Francisco look good together. And whoo, that boy can dance!"

Kanani giggles. "I know. He's hot."

"He likes you. I can see it in his eyes."

"Really?" For some reason, the thought makes Kanani's stomach fill with butterflies. "He's a sweet guy," she says. "Unlike some guys I could mention."

"That creep!" Rae says with feeling. Then she sighs. "I just wish we knew he was all right."

"I know what you mean. I'd feel horrible if something happened to him."

Visions of James being rescued by the Coast Guard—or worse, *not* being rescued—fill Kanani's head. Then a knock on the door brings her back to reality. "Come in," she calls.

Francisco pokes his head around the door and grins. *"Buenos días!"*

"Buenos días to you," Kanani replies. "Where'd you sleep last night?"

"On the sofa in the living room. Most people crashed on sleeping bags. A few stayed up all night."

"Are you serious?" Rae asks with a laugh.

He nods. "The batteries in the boom box died around three in the morning, but that didn't stop them. Rob and a couple other guys got out their guitars and made their own music."

Kanani's stomach emits a hungry growl. "I smell bacon," she declares.

"Rob's grandparents are making everyone breakfast," Francisco replies. "Better get up or you'll miss out."

That's all Kanani and Rae need to hear. They throw on their clothes and hurry into the hallway. The line for the bathroom stretches all the way to the living room! With a groan, they join it.

Later, the girls head for the kitchen. Rob's grandparents are serving up coffee, eggs, bacon, and toast. The shutters are open now and everything is bright and cheerful. The partygoers, looking tired but happy, sit on the living room floor, eating and chatting.

Then Rob's mother turns on the radio. The announcer is talking about the storm. Kanani catches the words *minimal damage* and *coastal flooding*.

"Did he say anything about injuries or deaths?" Rae asks anxiously.

"I don't know," she answers. "It's too noisy in here."

"You two about ready to go?" Francisco asked. "I want to get you back before your friend's parents call out the National Guard."

Kanani giggles, but the truth is she isn't looking forward to facing Tuck and Cate. Last night Cate sounded seriously ticked, and in the cold light of day, Kanani understands why. What she and Rae did wasn't very smart, she knows that now. It was their crush on James that made them want to sneak off. But the feeling's gone now, blown away with the hurricane.

They thank Rob and his family and go out to see how Francisco's van fared in the storm. They have to wade through six inches of water to get to it, but fortunately, the van starts right up and they drive away.

A1A is open. They cruise along, listening to one of Francisco's salsa tapes. Kanani's mind drifts back to last night. She remembers the feel of Francisco's arms around her and the way he softly whispered the salsa steps in her ear. She can almost smell his shampoo and feel his warm breath against her skin. The memory sends a pleasant shiver down her spine.

She sneaks a look at Francisco, only to discover he's looking at her. Blushing furiously, she turns away and concentrates instead on the gray, angry-looking ocean. Did James really go out in that insane surf? she wonders. Where did he spend the night? Is he okay?

"You mind if I stop by Uncle Luis's shop?" Francisco asks. "It'll only take a minute. I just want to make sure there was no serious damage."

"Sure," Kanani and Rae answer in unison.

Francisco drives off the highway and into Sebastian Inlet State Park. It's still officially closed, but the ranger waves him through. At the dock, they're relieved to see that the shop is still in one piece. Aside from some trash strewn around, the only damage is to the sign on the roof, which is listing at a forty-five-degree angle.

"Interesting," Francisco says, standing with his hands on his hips. "Maybe we should leave it that way."

"You can change the name of the place to Tower of Pisa Water Sports," Kanani quips.

Francisco laughs. "Oh, yeah. Uncle Luis would love that!"

"Don't look now," Rae says suddenly, "but you'll never guess what the storm washed up."

Kanani turns around to see James sauntering up the dock toward them, a big grin plastered across his face. "Hey, Francisco! Hi, girls. Did you see that surf yesterday afternoon? Double overhead, and I was chargin' it! Man, you should have seen me!"

"I can't believe you actually went out!" Kanani cries. "We were so worried about you!"

"Really?" James asks. "Why?"

"*Why?*" Rae gasps. "Didn't you hear the surf advisory? The waves were really dangerous. You could have been killed!"

"Not me. I'm invincible!" He puffs up his chest and shows off his biceps like Superman. Then he bursts out laughing.

Kanani can't believe his cocky attitude. "But where were you?" she asks. "We drove all the way down to Wabasso looking for you."

"I was farther south, at the Vero Beach Pier. You should have kept drivin'."

"We couldn't," Francisco says. "The streets were flooded and they closed A1A. We ended up spending the night at Rob Schiller's house."

"Well, then, it wasn't a total loss," James chuckles. "You probably got a free meal out of it."

"That's not the point," Rae tells him. "We went to a lot of trouble trying to find you, James. You could at least say thank you."

"Okay, okay, thank you," he says with a shrug. "Not that I needed finding. I mean, what's the big deal? I caught a few waves and then I drove to my grandmother's house in Belle Glade. End of story."

Rae's cheeks are turning red and she looks like she's about to explode. Kanani knows how she feels. It's not like she expects James to fall to his knees and kiss their feet, but he might at least show a tiny bit of gratitude. After all, they risked their own safety because they cared about his. So why is he acting so unconcerned?

What am I thinking? Kanani asks herself. *Unconcerned is James's middle name. If he cared about people, would he have strung Rae and me along the way he did? No way!*

"Hey, Francisco," James says, turning from Rae, "you feel like going jet-skiin'?"

Kanani can't believe it. James is so caught up in his

own little world, he hasn't even noticed that the jet skis are gone.

"Look around, man," Francisco says. "Uncle Luis and I loaded up all the vehicles and took them inland. Maybe you didn't notice, but we had a hurricane last night."

"Oh, right." James chuckles. "Well, maybe later. The waves are still pretty good out on the lagoon."

Kanani shakes her head. She wishes she could hammer some sense into James's head. Or at least show him he can't get away with treating people badly and breaking all the rules.

Suddenly, an idea pops into her head—a way to really put James in his place. If she can pull it off . . .

"I wish you *had* found me yesterday," James is crowing. "You could have bought one of those instant cameras and snapped some photos. I was really rippin'! It was like, unreal!"

Rae practically has steam coming out of her ears. "You *are* pretty unreal, J.T.," she growls. "I mean, the way you treated Kanani and—"

"Hey, Rae, I think we'd better be getting back, don't you?" Kanani breaks in.

"Not yet. I've got a few things to say to J.T. first."

"Save it for later," Kanani says, grabbing her friend's arm and practically dragging her down the dock. "Come on, Francisco."

"Where's the fire?" James calls, but Kanani doesn't stop walking until they reach the van.

"What was all that about?" Rae asks angrily. "I have a few things I want to say to that rat. Don't you?"

"Not yet," Kanani replies. "First, I have a question to ask you. That day when we were jet-skiing and you two went out without me, did James take you into the mangroves?"

Rae gnaws her fingernail and looks away. "Yes."

"What?" Francisco cries. "James knows darn well that jet skis disturb the wildlife in the mangroves. I've told him that a hundred times. That's just the kind of thoughtless behavior the coalition is trying to stop."

"He took me into the mangroves too," Kanani says. "I think it's about time someone showed him he can't get away with it. What do you think? Will you two help me nail him?"

"Totally!" Rae says.

"What's the plan?" Francisco asks with interest.

"Get in," Kanani says. "I'll tell you as we drive." She can feel herself snapping into Hawaiian Hurricane mode. "This is going to be fun."

16

*T*here they are," Kanani whispers, pointing. "You ready?"

"Ready as I'll ever be," Rae whispers back.

Up ahead, James and Francisco are sitting side by side on the edge of the dock. The sun is shining tentatively through the clouds.

"Hi, James!" Kanani and Rae coo in their best love-struck voices.

"Oh, hey, girls," James says, grinning as he gets to his feet. "Francisco tells me you're ready for another jet-ski lesson."

Gazing at James's lopsided smile and killer dimples, Kanani can almost convince herself she's still in love with him. All she has to do is remember how she used to feel before she found out he was a two-timing jerk.

"We'd love to go jet-skiing with you," she says sweetly. "If you have the time."

"Yes, you're such a wonderful teacher," Rae adds adoringly.

"Let's do it," James says, strutting to the jet skis. Kanani shoots Rae a conspiratorial smile. James is sucking up the girls' compliments like soda through a straw.

"Hey, Francisco, wanna come along?" James asks, climbing on the nearest jet ski.

"No, thanks, buddy," Francisco replies. "I have to keep an eye on the shop. You three enjoy yourselves."

Kanani and Rae each hop on a jet ski and start the engines. Soon James and the girls are cruising away from the dock and heading toward the lagoon.

Kanani guns the throttle and moves up beside him. "James," she asks, tipping her chin toward Rae, "do we have to spend the whole time with *her?*"

"Well, uh, we can't just drive off and leave her," he says uneasily.

"Why not? Don't you want to be alone with me?"

"Well, sure, but—"

"I'm the one you love, aren't I?" Kanani asks.

James glances at Rae, then back to Kanani. "Well, yeah, but—"

Now Rae cruises up on James's other side. "What are you two talking about?" she asks.

"Nothing," James says quickly.

142

"I wish you'd pay attention to me, J.T.," she says in a whiny voice.

"I am payin' attention, sugar."

"*Sugar?*" Kanani breaks in. "Why did you call her sugar?"

"It don't mean nothin'," James says. "It's just—"

"What do you mean, it don't mean nothin'?" Rae asks, mimicking him. "Don't you care about me?"

"Of course I do. It's just . . . it's just . . ."

"It's just *what?*" Kanani and Rae ask together.

James looks like a deer caught between two hungry mountain lions. "Well, will you look at that?" he exclaims, pointing vaguely toward the middle of the lagoon. Before the girls can say another word, he roars ahead of them.

Kanani cracks up. "That was sweet!"

"I love watching him squirm."

"We've got him so nervous, he doesn't know which way is up."

Rae checks her watch. "It's almost time," she announces.

Kanani nods knowingly. "Let's go."

Together, Kanani and Rae roar across the water until they catch up with James.

"J.T.," Rae asks, "will you take us into the mangroves?"

"I thought you wanted to learn more about jet-skiing," he says.

"We do," Kanani agrees. "But first we want to look for manatees. Please?"

"Yes, please, J.T.?" Rae adds, smiling sweetly.

"Well, okay. Why not? Follow me."

James zooms across the lagoon with the girls close behind. Soon, the mangrove swamp appears in the distance. Overhead, an egret flies by, its long wings flapping gracefully.

James leads them into the twisting maze of mangroves. "Don't we have to slow down?" Rae asks. "I wouldn't want to hit a manatee or something."

He shrugs. "Those manatee are bigger than we are. They can look out for themselves."

"That's not true," Kanani blurts out. "Francisco told me that the leading cause of manatee deaths is from boat collisions. And it isn't just propeller boats either. Manatees usually travel at a speed of three to five miles per hour, so any boat traveling faster than fifteen or twenty—even a jet ski—can hurt or kill a manatee."

Rae shoots Kanani a warning look and Kanani winces. She's not supposed to be criticizing James; she's supposed to be buttering him up.

Fortunately, James doesn't seem concerned. He snorts a laugh and says, "Francisco has too much time on his hands. What that boy needs is a girlfriend." He turns down a narrow passage between two rows of mangroves. "Keep your eyes peeled. This is where we saw the manatee last time."

"Rae told me all about the time you two came here without me," Kanani says, slipping back into the role of jealous girlfriend. It was a role she'd once played for real. But now, no way! "Why did you do that, James?"

"Isn't it obvious?" Rae pipes up. "J.T. loves me best."

"That isn't true, is it, James?" Kanani demands.

James is wriggling like a worm on a hook. He forces a chuckle and says, "Girls, don't fight. There's plenty of me to go around."

Kanani and Rae exchange a look. It's time to stop pretending. They reach into the pockets of their board shorts and pull out the fake gold coins. "I guess there are plenty of these to go around too," Kanani declares.

James's jaw drops. "I . . . I can explain."

"Go ahead," Rae says. "Let's hear it."

"Well, um, you see, I found two coins," he stammers. "And, well, I didn't want either of you to feel left out, so . . . er . . . uh . . ."

Suddenly, from around a bend in the mangroves, a WaveRunner appears. The driver is a burly state park ranger with a dark beard. His passenger is Francisco.

"Good morning, J.T.," the park ranger calls. "How are you doing today?"

James's face falls. "I was better before I saw you," he mutters.

"Seems to me I've warned you three or four times to stay out of the mangroves with that jet ski," the ranger says. "Guess now I'm going to have to give you a ticket." He writes out the ticket and hands it to James.

"Fifty dollars!" James gasps. "Oh, come on!"

"Maybe this time you'll listen," the ranger says.

"Well, what about the girls?" James cries indignantly. "They're here too, aren't they? Why aren't you busting them?"

"Because they're tourists and don't know any better," Francisco pipes up. "As a matter of fact, the only reason they're here is because you told them it was all right."

"Is that true?" the ranger asks.

"No!" James cries.

"Yes," Kanani and Rae say innocently.

The ranger looks from James to the girls and back again. "Well, if it's their word against yours, J.T. Tibbets, I guess I'll believe them."

James shoots Francisco an angry look. "Thanks a lot, dude. I thought you were my friend."

"I try to be," Francisco says, "but you make it awfully hard sometimes."

James curses under his breath and looks away.

"What's that?" the ranger asks.

"Nothing," James practically spits.

"That's what I thought." The ranger smiles. "Have a nice day, folks." Then he turns the WaveRunner around and drives away. As he disappears around the bend, Francisco looks over his shoulder and waves.

"You were in on that, weren't you?" James growls, glaring at Kanani and Rae. "You set me up."

Kanani just smiles. "Next time you want to play two girls off each other, I suggest you pick ones who are more gullible."

"And who aren't such good friends," Rae adds.

Kanani nods. "We West Coast surfer girls are smart. And we stick together."

"Yeah," James grumbles, "and you talk too much too."

Kanani laughs. "Let's go, Rae. We've got better things to do than to hang out with this loser."

She tosses her coin at James. Rae tosses hers too. He grabs for them, but they fall into the water with a plop.

"Guess you'll have to buy some new ones before you can pull that scam again," Kanani remarks.

"Hey, J.T.," Rae calls as they turn the jet skis around, "if you're ever in California, do us a favor and don't look us up!"

"Oh, yeah?" he sputters. "Well, I . . . uh, I . . ."

James is still trying to think up a snappy comeback as the girls hit the throttle and drive away, showering him with their spray.

17

*I*s this yours, Luna?" Kanani asks, holding up a damp bathing suit top she found under the bed.

Luna looks up from the corner of the motel room where she's sitting cross-legged on the floor with David. The two of them have been like that for the last half hour, their foreheads practically touching, talking intently.

"Oh, yeah. Thanks," Luna replies, but she's only half there. Kanani tosses her the bathing suit top and Luna refocuses her gaze on David.

They're so in love, Kanani thinks. *I can practically see little pink hearts floating above their heads.*

She sighs. Oh, how she longs to find a love like that! Instead, she found James Tibbets.

Not exactly true love, she thinks with an inward groan, *but definitely a learning experience.*

Kanani zips up her bag and gazes out the window. Unexpectedly, Francisco's face appears in her mind. How different he is from James! Not as handsome or charismatic maybe, but oh, so much kinder and more dependable. And real. Unlike James, he's someone Kanani knows she can trust.

She smiles, thinking it over. Maybe her relationship with James wasn't a *total* disaster. After all, if it wasn't for him, she and Francisco never would have become friends.

But is that all there is between us? Kanani wonders. She thinks back to the hurricane party. When Francisco held her in his arms and they moved together to the hot salsa music, she felt a buzz that even James's kisses couldn't match. But was it just the excitement of the party that made the moment seem so special? Or is there something more between them—something worth pursuing?

Suddenly, Kanani knows she has to find out. With new purpose, she grabs her bag and lugs it outside to the parking lot. Tuck is loading up the SUV while Cate checks the map.

"When do we leave for the airport?" Kanani asks.

"We still have a few hours before we have to check in," Tuck replies. "I thought we'd stop by the inlet for a quick surf session. How's that sound?"

"Sweet!" she cries, and it's not just the chance to catch one more Sebastian Inlet grinder that's got her stoked. It's Francisco. She'd thought maybe she could call him, but how much better is this? She can hardly wait to see him again!

"Aren't you going surfing?" Cate asks incredulously.

Tuck has just taken the boards off the SUV and the girls are waxing up before heading into the water. Even David is going out, eager to renew his surfing skills among the still formidable waves. But Kanani has laid her board on the sand and is standing with her back to the ocean.

"I'll go out in a few minutes," she says. "I'm going for a walk first."

Cate shoots her a warning glance. "Just promise me you won't hop in a taxi and disappear like you did last time."

Kanani smiles sheepishly. "I promise."

"Okay. Have fun."

Kanani jogs across the bridge and over to the dock. She finds Francisco with his back to her, crouching over one of the powerboat's outboard motors. She walks closer, her heart racing like a jet ski on full throttle.

On a whim, she covers Francisco's eyes with her hands. "Guess who?" she says in a silly, high-pitched voice.

Francisco lets out a weary sigh. "Bianca, come on! Can't you see I've got work to do?"

Kanani freezes. Does Francisco have a girlfriend? Oh, how embarrassing! Suddenly she longs to slip between the planks of the dock and disappear.

Francisco peels her hands from his eyes and spins around. "Kanani!" he exclaims, breaking into a grin. "I thought you were my niece. That little troublemaker has been hassling me all morning."

Kanani is so relieved she feels like hugging him. Instead, she says, "We're leaving for the airport in a couple of hours. I . . . I wanted to stop by and say good-bye."

"Today?" His face falls. "But they've rescheduled the contest for next weekend. Can't you stay?"

Kanani shakes her head. "Tuck and Cate have to get back to the surf shop." She shrugs. "The funny thing is, I'm not all that upset about missing the contest. I was at first, but in the end I thought better of it. This trip has been rewarding in so many other ways. I got to travel far from home to another beautiful place on the U.S. coastline. I've made new friends. Plus, I still got in a lot of surf time. In the end, I guess I'm a lot like Tuck—a dyed-in-the-wool soul-surfer. Competing just isn't that important to me."

"But then how will you get to Hawaii?" Francisco asks. "I thought you were hoping to attract a sponsor who would send you there."

"I'll find a way eventually. There will be other contests. Right now, I'm not sure I'm ready yet. Those

North Shore waves are really heavy. I've got a lot of surfing to do before I can paddle out with the locals."

Francisco puts down the wrench he's holding and sits on the edge of the dock. Motioning Kanani to join him, he says, "T-Bone is still steaming about that fine the ranger gave him. He says he's going to challenge it."

"But how? The ranger caught him red-handed."

"He'll make up a story about how he was trying to rescue a wounded manatee or some rubbish like that. That dude can really shovel the bull when he wants to."

Kanani giggles. "I learned that firsthand."

"Yeah, I guess you did," Francisco says seriously. "Maybe I should have warned you about him. I guess I just figured you hip California girls could handle yourselves. But maybe if I'd spoken up . . . well, no, it never would have happened."

"What? What wouldn't have happened?"

"Kanani, I liked you from the moment I laid eyes on you. But I knew you'd never pick me over a good-looking guy like T-Bone. Nobody ever does."

Kanani can feel her heart flutter in her chest. "I was dazzled by James," she admits. "I guess most girls are. But I'm seeing things a lot more clearly now. There's only one Florida boy I care about." By now her heart is pounding so hard she can barely hear herself whisper the word, "You."

Francisco looks at her, his chocolate brown eyes glistening. Then he takes her in his arms and kisses her. Kanani kisses back, and as she does, she feels a warm glow radiating inside her. It's like swallowing sunshine, and it's completely different from the jumpy, jangly electricity she felt when she kissed James.

Is this what love feels like? Kanani wonders. She's not sure. All she knows is that she wants to keep feeling it forever.

Suddenly, from somewhere behind her, Kanani hears a tiny giggle. She and Francisco pull apart and turn toward the rental shop. A young girl, maybe six or seven years old, is watching them with her hand over her mouth.

"Bianca!" Francisco says. "Go away! This is private!"

"Then why are you doing it right here on the dock?"

He shakes his head and laughs. "Get gone, girl. Go buy yourself a candy bar." He hands her some coins and she runs off, giggling happily.

"I'd better go too," Kanani says. "Rae and I are already in hot water with Tuck and Cate for running off during the hurricane. I don't want them to think I ran off again."

"I meant to ask you what happened with that," Francisco says.

"Our punishment is that we have to work fifty hours without pay at Tuck and Cate's surf shop," she replies.

"Doesn't sound too bad to me."

"Me either. I love hanging around their shop. But wait until my parents find out what we did. They'll probably ground me until I graduate from high school."

"I hope they'll let you send an e-mail once in a while. I'd like to keep in touch."

Kanani smiles. "For sure. And who knows? Maybe someday we'll travel to Hawaii together."

"And Cuba," he adds. "You haven't tasted real garlic chicken until you've had it at my great-aunt Lupe's house in Havana."

"I'd like that," she says.

But Francisco isn't listening. He's staring at something beyond the edge of the dock. "Shh," he says, holding his finger to his lips. "Come here."

Kanani takes a step forward and looks down. A manatee is swimming slowly through the shallow water! She watches as its hulking body disappears beneath the dock.

"Now you can tell your friends back in California you saw a real Florida manatee," Francisco declares.

Kanani can hardly believe her eyes! It was amazing enough seeing the sea turtle with James, but this is even better because she's with someone she really cares about, someone who loves nature as much as she does. "Thank you," she whispers, standing on tiptoe to kiss Francisco's cheek.

"For what?" he asks.

"For making this a trip I'll never forget."

There's a ballpoint pen sticking out of the pocket of Francisco's T-shirt. Kanani takes it, reaches for his hand, and writes her e-mail address on his palm. "Write to me," she tells him.

He takes back the pen and smiles at her. "I will, Kanani. You know I will."

Back at First Peak, Kanani's friends are catching some sweet little rides. She paddles out to join them.

"Where were you?" Rae asks.

"Saying good-bye to Francisco."

"Something happened between you two," Luna teases. "I can tell by that moony look on your face. Did he kiss you?"

Kanani just grins.

"They've got the major hots for each other," Rae explains. "I could tell when I watched them dance together at the hurricane party." She touches Kanani's shoulder and makes a sizzling sound.

"Call the fire department," Luna says. She wails like a siren and flings a handful of water at Kanani's face. Kanani shrieks and splashes back, and soon all three girls are having a wild water fight. David paddles over and joins in. It doesn't end until the girls shove him off his surfboard. He hits the water with a plop.

David climbs back on his board and gazes lovingly at Luna. "I don't want to go home."

Kanani thinks of Francisco and her heart aches. She doesn't want to leave him—not now, when she's just getting to know him. But in another way, she's eager to go home. She misses her family. She didn't think she would, but she does. She can't wait to taste her mother's blueberry pancakes, play chess with her father, and shoot hoops with Cameron.

But first, there's one more thing she has to do. She needs to ride some ripping Sebastian Inlet waves. Looking over her shoulder, she sees a set coming in. She starts paddling. Beside her, Rae is paddling too.

It's Kanani's wave, but she wants to share it. "Let's ride together!" she calls.

They drop in and stand up. Side by side, they sail across the face of the wave. Then suddenly, Rae steps off her board and hops on behind Kanani.

"Whoa!" Kanani cries, struggling to keep her balance.

Rae puts her hands on Kanani's hips, steadying her. Now they're riding together, laughing so hard they can barely stand up.

Suddenly, the wave collides with a Second Peak breaker. The girls fly off the board, squealing and laughing. They pop up side by side and slap each other a high five.

"Kanani," Rae says, suddenly serious, "let's never fight over a boy again."

"Never. Our friendship is more important."

"You know it, girlfriend."

Kanani feels so happy, she almost believes she could fly out to the lineup. "Let's catch another," she says.

Rae nods and they paddle back out through the sparkling blue waves of Sebastian Inlet together.

LUNA BAY

Roxy Shopping Spree Sweepstakes

OFFICIAL RULES:

1. No purchase necessary.

2. To enter, complete the official entry form or hand print your name, address, and phone number along with the words "Roxy Shopping Spree Sweepstakes" on a 3" x 5" card and mail to: HarperEntertainment, 10 E. 53rd Street, New York, NY 10022. Entries must be received by October 1, 2003. Enter as often as you wish, but each entry must be mailed separately. One entry per envelope. Partially completed, illegible, or mechanically reproduced entries will not be accepted. Sponsors are not responsible for lost, late, mutilated, illegible, stolen, postage due, incomplete, or misdirected entries. All entries become the property of HarperCollins and will not be returned.

3. Sweepstakes are open to all legal residents of the United States (excluding residents of Colorado and Rhode Island), who are between the ages of eight and sixteen by October 1, 2003, excluding employees and immediate family members of HarperCollins, Roxy, and Quiksilver, Inc., and their respective subsidiaries, and affiliates, officers, directors, shareholders, employees, agents, attorneys, and other representatives (individually and collectively), and their respective parent companies, affiliates, subsidiaries, advertising, promotion and fulfillments agencies, and the persons with whom each of the above are domiciled. Offer void where prohibited or restricted.

4. Odds of winning depend on total number of entries received. Approximately 100,000 entry forms distributed. All prizes will be awarded. Winners will be randomly drawn on or about October 15, 2003, by representatives of HarperCollins, whose decisions are final. Potential winners will be notified by mail and a parent or guardian of the potential winner will be required to sign and return an affidavit of eligibility and release of liability within fourteen days of notification. Failure to return affidavit within time period will disqualify winner, and another winner will be chosen. By acceptance of prize, winner consents to the use of his or her name, photographs, likeness, and personal information by HarperCollins, Roxy, and Quiksilver, Inc., for publicity and advertising purposes without further compensation except where prohibited.

5. One (1) Grand Prize winner will receive a $500 gift certificate redeemable through Roxy.com. HarperCollins reserves the right at its sole discretion to substitute another prize of equal or of greater value in the event prize is unavailable. Approximate retail value $500.00.

6. Only one prize will be awarded per individual, family, or household. Prizes are nontransferable and cannot be sold or redeemed for cash. No cash substitute is available except at the sole discretion of HarperCollins for reasons of prize unavailability. Any federal, state, or local taxes are the responsibility of the winner.

7. Additional terms: By participating, entrants agree a) to the official rules and decisions of the judges, which will be final in all respects; and b) to release, discharge, and hold harmless HarperCollins, Roxy, and Quiksilver, Inc., and their affiliates, subsidiaries, and advertising promotion agencies from and against any and all liability or damages associated with acceptance, use, or misuse of any prize received in this sweepstakes.

8. To obtain the name of the winners, please send your request and a self-addressed stamped envelope (Vermont residents may omit return postage) to "Roxy Winners List" c/o HarperEntertainment, 10 E. 53rd Street, New York, NY 10022.

SPONSOR: HarperCollins Publishers Inc.

TM & © 2003 Roxy, A division of Quiksilver, Inc